# THE SACRIFICE

KITTY THOMAS

BURLESQUE PRESS

# S THE
# ACRIFICE

## KITTY THOMAS

*Burlesque Press*

# 1

## MACY

I've tried to deny it, but I've always known this was my fate. In certain families there are duties, and some of those duties are more unsavory than others. I've been kept pure for this, and tonight, I am their sacrifice.

I'm led blindfolded down a long hallway and through a door that creaks ominously as we pass through. My breath catches when I hear the men. I can't see them, but I've been prepared for this. I know what to expect.

They're young—ten of them, all close to my age. We went to private school together. The oldest is five years older than me. They are the future titans of industry, and they're here to fulfill their duty—to impregnate me and continue tradition. And may the strongest sperm win.

The blindfold comes off, but I keep my eyes cast down on the floor. My naked body is barely covered by a white cloak that ties at the neck and then a couple of places beneath that so my modesty is protected. My modesty. Such a joke. No one will care about my modesty as soon as the initial formalities are over.

There's another man, this one older—one of the fathers: Mr. Kingston. We'll call him the Master of Ceremonies.

"Do you understand why you're here, Macy?"

"Y-yes, Sir."

"I'm glad you were prepared for this, though tradition requires me to explain it to you anyway."

Of course it does.

The coming narrative isn't for my benefit. It's for the benefit of the young men here, who will each get to touch me, taste me, claim me, bury their seed inside me in an attempt to be the victor. I will marry whoever is successful, whoever's heir I end up carrying, which will be determined by paternity test. I can't even begin to imagine how this was done before modern technology.

Maybe the ritual was different then.

"Each of these young men will please you. You are *required* to come for each of them. Do you understand, Macy?"

"Y-yes, Mr. Kingston."

"Sir was just fine," he says, his stern forest green eyes boring through me so that I find myself looking back down at the ground.

"Yes, Sir."

"Good girl. After that you'll be allowed a break. The entire ritual will take hours, you see, and we wouldn't want you to get light headed from hunger. Each of them will fuck you, and you are once again required to come for them. All of them. We'll know if you're faking. What happens if you fake or if you fail to come for them, Macy?"

"P-punishment, Sir." My face is hot, flaming, but the place between my legs flames more.

"That's right, Macy. Punishment. And we want this to all be about pleasure, don't we?"

"Yes, Sir."

Mysterious hands seem to come from nowhere to untie the cords that hold the cloak in place. Then the lush fabric is pushed from my shoulders to land in a pile at my feet. This entire speech is for the entertainment of the spoiled rich men who are about to enjoy their sacrifice. Though I will enjoy it, too. It was designed for my pleasure, after all.

Though I've been told it isn't really about my pleasure but about ensuring a pregnancy results from the ritual. Orgasms open the cervix. And I'm ovulating, so this is happening now. I'll be carrying the child of one of these men tonight. Fate will decide who I'll spend the rest of my life with, based only on the strongest swimmer.

I know every single moment of what's supposed to transpire. I know every move, every part of this ritual by heart. Mr. Kingston raises an eyebrow at me, his look expectant. In response, I take a deep breath and drop to my knees. I crawl slowly to him, and suddenly every eye in the room is on me. Previously the men had been scattered about, drinks in hands, low murmurs as they pretended to talk to each other, as they pretended I was beneath their notice. But they can't pretend anymore.

"Good girl."

A gasp escapes my throat as I feel his hand stroke through my hair and then move around to cup my breast. I thought only the guys my age would touch me.

Two of the men help me to my feet and guide me onto a table where I'll be examined by the doctor to ensure my purity is intact before it's destroyed in this one long orgy.

A phone rings, breaking my focus. Dammit. I was so close. The fantasy drifts away, and with it, any hope of an orgasm this morning. I roll over in bed to find Livia's name flashing on my cell phone screen.

"It's eight in the morning. You know that's my *me* time," I grumble when I answer. And she knows exactly what I mean by that. Other people have their morning coffee, I have my morning orgasm. This has been my go-to fantasy for months now. It hits all the buttons: exhibitionism. Multiple men. Lots of orgasms. The *demand* of orgasms. Helpless, vulnerable, arousal. And I'm working myself up again now just thinking of the elements of this perfect spank fantasy.

"Sorry," Livia says. But she doesn't sound that sorry. This daily appointment with pleasure isn't as sacred to her as it is to me, obviously.

She giggles in the background, and I hear rumbling male voices. Those would be her three... husbands? Is that what we're calling them? Only one is legally married to her in the sense that they went and got a marriage license and had a wedding. The other two have private business contracts that are basically the same as marriage without calling it marriage. Apparently as long as nobody calls it marriage it's not polygamy—at least not technically. I think. I don't know. I'm not a lawyer. Maybe it's still polygamy, or at the very least adultery. I need to research this because it's going to bug me.

"I thought we were going dress shopping today. It's your turn!" Livia sounds way more excited about this than I feel.

My best friend has been married for the past three months. Even though I caught the bouquet at her wedding, I didn't believe I'd be next because I wasn't even dating anyone. Then two months ago this guy I was friends with in college popped back into my life.

One night while drunk, we'd made this silly pact that if we weren't married by the time we were thirty, we'd marry each other. And when he called in this pact, I couldn't come up with a good reason why I shouldn't do it—aside from the fact that it's crazy, and drunken promises to marry someone you barely know if you happen to be single in a decade is hardly the kind of thing normal people expect you to follow through on.

William is nice. He's nice enough looking. He's got a stable job. And I really want kids. I've still got some time on the baby clock, but I don't see how the next ten years will be more fruitful for dating than the last ten were. I don't even know how to date in the land of the perpetual player. And I've got a bit of an awkward problem.

I'm almost thirty and still a virgin. Yeah, that part of the fantasy is real. I know I shouldn't be ashamed of it, but I am. It makes me feel like I'm some kind of loser who didn't have any opportunities—like no man wanted me. And I've walked through the local grocery store. I've seen pregnancies that defy all sexual attraction explanation.

But that isn't it. A lot of guys have tried to sleep with me. I just didn't because I wanted them to still be there the next day, and I could tell I was just a conquest—a curiosity. I've never been gifted with that ability to lie to myself that maybe this guy is *the one* when I know he isn't.

There's also that situation when you're in that zone where it's still totally normal to be a virgin, lots of other people your age are, and then suddenly everybody else has done the deed and you're still standing there, suddenly out of the loop. It felt like I went from *this is totally normal* to *it's getting kind of weird* almost overnight. Then I just stayed there. Like I'd somehow accidentally taken a vow in a convent, and that was that. Sorry, too late now, best to accept your spinsterhood. Here's your free starter cat!

Most good men are freaked out by my late-stage virginity as though it's a red flag all by itself. Or they don't want the responsibility of being my first. It's too much pressure. Only the bad men really like it.

And I'm just so shy and awkward.

I'm always researching everything and know weird facts

about everything, and I mean, that's kind of strange for dating. Right? And I don't have that thing. You know that thing? The sexy airy breezy way some women have about them? That power over men. That *siren* thing. That certain *je ne sais qua*. I don't have it. Though I've googled how to get it, to little avail. Everybody makes it sound so easy, but it just isn't so easy for me. I'm not like that, and I just feel fake and awkward when I try. But I want to be that woman in my imagination so much I can barely stand it.

"Macy, did you just stroke out or something? You have to have a dress. You're getting married in six months."

I resist the urge to say *Don't remind me.*

"Do you think he's gay?" I blurt out.

"What?!?" Livia laughs out loud on her answer.

"I mean... why is he in such a rush to get married? And he hasn't tried to sleep with me. We are getting *married* and he hasn't pushed for sex once. That's weird, right? I want to call it off."

"I don't think he's gay," Livia says. "He's just shy. And he knows you haven't... Maybe he thinks you're religious, and he's trying to respect your boundaries."

"That pisses me off," I say.

"That he's respecting your boundaries?"

"No. That he might think it's because of religion. Also, my skirts are a little short for fundamentalism. Don't you think?"

I'm about two seconds from launching into an extreme, likely thirty-minute rant about how the way I am is how almost *all* women used to be. I mean, not obsessively researching arcane random facts, but the chaste until marriage thing. That used to be normal. I don't want this one more thing to make me feel *abnormal*. I already feel abnormal enough.

Then I start crying. I don't know where this is coming

from. I mean I do, but I was fine a minute ago. Fine-*ish*. And now I'm sobbing over the phone like I'm about to be thrown into a volcano instead of getting married to a nice enough, good looking enough, and financially secure enough man.

"Macy?" Livia sounds concerned.

"I don't want to marry him." The words come out in a rush, more blubbering than speech. And then I get into a pathetic hiccuping sob where I can't fully catch my breath, and I sound like a two year old having a meltdown over no ice cream for dinner.

We've booked the venue. We've got deposits down on everything. I'm sure this is why I don't have a dress yet, why the idea is giving me stress acne instead of making me feel excited. I don't want to marry this guy. I don't feel anything for him. And I just know he'll be missionary position lights out guy. I can't spend my *life* with missionary position lights out guy. I mean look at my fantasies!

This is probably another reason I'm still a virgin. I don't know how to ask for what I need or want. And even if I could say the words, even if I could let a man in on my twisted mind, there just aren't any men I can trust enough for that. How would I ever do the things I want to do with anyone? I've never even been naked with a man before. And I don't know how I'll ever be able to bring myself to do even that. I can't picture it in my mind at all—being naked with a guy. I can picture it when I'm fantasizing, but I mean... I can't see it as a possible real activity that I could ever actually engage in. It's all just so... impossible.

I should call off the wedding, get some cats, and just call it done.

And I feel so stupid even thinking these things. At least I'm not saying them out loud. That would be worse.

My mind, body, and experience are not at all in alignment. I don't think anybody would guess that behind my bookish nerdy glasses are some very dark and wrong thoughts.

I mean it is so me to be a virgin trying to figure out how to get super kinky sex when I haven't even done it the regular way yet. You have to crawl before you can walk after all. No kinky puns intended. The whole situation embarrasses me.

"If you don't want to marry him you should tell him now before this goes any further. You haven't even ordered the invitations."

"All those deposits are nonrefundable," I say, flopping back on the bed as though I've suddenly been transported to the Victorian era. I'm a millisecond away from dramatically putting my hand to my forehead in distress.

"So? Is it worth sacrificing your life over? I can give you the money back if you need it."

I know she's right. And anyway it's not like it would be that much embarrassment on my end—calling things off, I mean. What little family I have, I'm not in contact with. The only people I was planning to invite to the wedding are Livia, her guys, and her family. I don't even know who to put in my wedding besides Livia. This whole thing makes me feel like I'm living a lie. I'm planning a wedding for a woman who doesn't exist. I wish she existed, I want to be her, but I don't know how to get there from here.

"Just come pick me up," I say on a sigh. "We'll go look at the dresses. I can at least try some on." And fantasize about a dream wedding to a man I actually want to marry.

"Are you sure? It was just a stupid pact. Nobody follows that *if we aren't married by thirty we marry each other* shit. Nobody. It's just a thing you say. Macy, you don't have to marry him. You know that, right?"

Don't I though? He feels like the last boat—the only boat that's coming. And I'm afraid if I don't do this I'll die alone.

IT's late in the afternoon when I collapse on the sofa, dropping my bags beside me. I got a dress. It's green. Not pale green. Dark green. And I'm not wearing a veil. I can't bring myself to wear a white dress because I'll feel like I have a flashing neon sign over my head announcing my purity to the world.

Anyway, the white dress isn't as traditional as people think. Queen Victoria started the tradition in 1840. Before that, nobody wore white. They just wore their nicest dress, whatever that was. I'm starting to wish I hadn't read every book I could find on weddings when we were planning Livia's. I can't escape these million stupid facts all swirling around in my brain as though they mean something—like they're important.

I jump at the sudden knock on my door.

"Who is it?" I call from the sofa. I'm not expecting anybody, and if someone's delivering pizza to the wrong apartment, I'd rather not get up.

"Soren."

I bolt upright. Soren is Livia's husband. The legal one. What's he doing here?

"Livia isn't here," I call back, still not moving.

"Could you open the door, please? I'm here to talk to you."

I struggle to get off the sofa, stopping to look in a mirror near the door. As expected, my long dark auburn curls are disheveled, and I can see the blush already starting in my cheeks, edging out the freckles dotting over my nose. I hate those freckles. I already look too innocent. Freckles are just a bridge too far in adorableness.

When I open the door, Soren sweeps right in without an invitation, smelling of whiskey and cigar smoke. I don't think I've ever seen him smoke a cigar, but he still smells that way. It's like that's just his natural masculine scent.

I can barely stand upright in this man's presence. Soren has a strong effect on me. I spent the entire time around Livia's wedding trying to focus my attention on Griffin, so I wouldn't be lusting after my best friend's soon-to-be husband. I didn't know at the time that Griffin was hers too. So it was a pointless waste of effort on my part. I put absolutely everything into that Oscar-worthy performance and made every effort not to even *look* at Soren. His pull was far too strong.

Then when I walked in on her and Griffin kissing, thinking she was cheating on the man I'd wanted... I locked myself in my car and had a long pathetic cry about it.

Soren is tall with dark forest green eyes and a body sculpted by the gods. But it isn't his looks or even his money that I'm so attracted to. It's his presence. The sheer dominant overpowering and terrifying essence that is Soren Kingston. Yeah, he's the *Mr. Kingston* in my longstanding fantasy. I make it okay in my head by aging him a couple of decades and not letting him participate. Much. Don't judge me.

He's like a storm that you just know will blow through and rip you apart from the inside out, but you're so enthralled watching it coming your way, you can't make yourself move out of the path of devastation in time.

"Do you have anything to drink?" he asks.

I still don't know why he's here, and I'm sure I'm so turned on he can tell. I wish I could turn this feeling off. I would never betray Livia—not that Soren would be into someone like me. But even if he was, I'd never hurt her. I just can't shut off my body's reaction to this man.

"Y-yeah. I-I have some tea. D-do you want tea?" Oh god, why am I stuttering? And I'm sure he means like a *drink*

drink, like an adult beverage, but I don't really keep liquor in the house. I'm not much of a drinker, and it's a small studio apartment so it's not like I do a lot of entertaining here.

"That'll be fine. Make some for yourself, too."

It's a command, and I swear if he were single I would strip off my clothes and kneel at his feet right now. I've never felt this way around a man before. I have no idea how Livia managed to go months without sleeping with him. Is it possible I feel a stronger attraction to her husband than she does? That would be tragic.

I wish he'd leave. What's he doing in my apartment? I take a deep breath and force my mind to stop racing as I heat the water in the kettle.

"Earl Grey or English Breakfast?" I hear myself say. It doesn't even sound like my own voice. It sounds far too high pitched and squeaky to be me. Or maybe it's more breathy like Marilyn Monroe.

"Whatever you're making for yourself is fine."

We're both silent in the kitchen. He stands several feet away, but it's still too close. In moments like this I'm jealous of Livia. I love her like a sister, but why does she get everything? She didn't just get one hot, wealthy, kinky guy. She got three. How is that even possible? It's statistically very unlikely. It just isn't fair. Meanwhile I'm about to marry a probably gay guy where I might get to have vanilla sex one time for the sake of procreation.

Lucky me.

Am I really going to marry him? Even though I'm going through the motions I'm still not sure I'll be able to go through with it. Livia's right though, I need to end things before the invitations get ordered. But why the hell did I buy a dress if I don't plan to actually marry him?

And I really thought we were to a point where a man could be gay and just be open about it. Why hide behind me and pretend? But then I remember that not literally everyone in the world is up to date on this, so maybe there's a reason he needs to hide. And I can feel sympathy for that, but it's still not right to hide behind me.

When the teapot whistles, I pour the tea into two cups and place them on the table. I can't stop thinking about how bizarre it is that Soren is standing in my apartment. And he still hasn't told me why he's here.

"Do you take milk and sugar?" I ask, desperate to fill the silence with anything but the sound of my raging heartbeat.

"Just milk."

I go to the fridge for the milk, wondering if he's planning some kind of surprise for Livia and wants my help. I leave the milk on the table, then grab the sugar for myself and some tea cookies out of the pantry. When I return, Soren is seated at the table, milk in his tea, already drinking.

I put sugar and milk in mine and take a couple of sips.

"So, why are you here again?" I ask. I'm sure I sound rude. I don't mean to, but I need him out of here before he figures out how much I wish I could be with him. I mean I don't have a crush or anything. I'm not in love with him. I just... he makes me feel like I'm in heat, and I kind of want to climb him like a tree.

"Are you nervous about something, Macy?"

I take a big gulp of my tea and then another. It's barely cool enough to be chugging it back like this, but I need a distraction.

"What would I be nervous about?"

"Let's not play games. I've seen how you react to me. You think I don't notice how you blush when I'm near? I think there's something dark and a little dirty in you. You probably have needs you've never even admitted to yourself."

The heat that was concentrated in my cheeks spreads

swiftly through the rest of my body. *Oh, I've admitted them to myself, but thank you for that psychoanalysis.*

"You're married," is all I can say. Is he propositioning me? If this bastard is propositioning me I will geld him.

Soren laughs. "You're so adorable."

I'm about to speak again but my tongue feels... weird. I can't make words work anymore. Soren's face blurs in front of me. Then the world tips to the side and goes black.

# 2

---

# MACY

I wake in a darkened room with a pounding headache. I can tell it's still day outside because heavy drapes cover the windows with light peeking in around the edges. I struggle to sit up in the bed, trying to remember how I got here. What happened last? I feel like I'm reading a sequel to a book where it's been so long since the first one came out that I don't remember the original plot.

I was talking to Soren over tea. What was it he wanted to talk to me about? I don't think he ever said. This is when the pieces begin to click together in a lumbering fuzzy sort of way. He *drugged* me. Why would he drug me? I try to get up, and the rest of my brain finally comes online as I feel the resistance and discover one of my wrists is handcuffed to the headboard of the bed.

I frantically search in the dim room for bolts I can unscrew to take the headboard apart. I have this sudden sharp clarity and vision in my head of how I can dismantle the headboard, slip the handcuff out, and find a way to escape. Except that I can't. This isn't some bag of bolts from a big box store. It's a nice bed. It was made as one piece, not a million that can be easily taken apart by a couple of drunk college students.

And then another troubling reality makes its way into my awareness. I'm naked under the covers. He took my clothes off? What is going on? Did he... did he touch me? I squeeze my eyes shut trying to block out that possibility.

"Hey! Soren, let me out of here! You motherfucker!" I can't believe I was attracted to this piece of shit. And now I'm starting to really fear for Livia's safety with this guy.

There's a vase of fresh flowers on the nightstand just within my reach. I take it with my free hand and hurl it across the room. The shattering of the vase is loud and satisfying even as it hurts my ears.

A moment later the door opens and Soren bursts in.

"What the fuck is this?" I shout. Even though he drugged me and kidnapped me and undressed me, I know this guy. I've known him nearly a year so it's hard for me to conjure up the normal fear response that this situation might otherwise create. I mean I'm pretty sure my life isn't in peril. And my body's still reacting to him like he's Christmas, which makes me feel so ashamed I wish I could melt through the mattress to hide under the bed.

He raises an eyebrow at me. "That's a very naughty word to come out of such a sweet mouth."

He glances at the shattered vase nonchalantly, but I can see the storm brewing inside him, that dangerous thing I'm so inappropriately attracted to.

Soren crosses the room to me and sits in a chair near the bed. "I'm afraid we're in a bit of a situation, and you've become the sacrifice."

"Are you going to throw me into a volcano?" It's meant to sound sarcastic and angry, but it comes out small and weak as though I think that might be what's really about to happen here. And honestly I'm not sure because who talks like this? *You've become the sacrifice?* What sacrifice? And suddenly I'm back inside my fantasy again, except this time it's a nightmare.

This feels like some kind of punishment for fantasizing about my best friend's husband.

He chuckles. "No, Macy. Though you'd be an appropriate candidate for a volcano god."

My eyes widen at this remark. Does he know I'm a virgin? How could he possibly know that? That's private. Would Livia have told him? She wouldn't. Or is it just that obvious how innocent I am? He's so perceptive he can probably smell the purity on me. I wonder what purity smells like. Gardenias? Crisp fresh sheets? A mountain spring?

Soren must read the betrayal on my face because he says, "Don't worry, Livia didn't tell me, but I know everything that happens in my home."

I wonder briefly if he's got the place wired up so he can spy on her, and once again I'm worried about my best friend's safety and once again wanting to disconnect this guy's balls from his body. Not only am I a sex fiend in my imaginary world, but quite violent as well.

I'm grateful the room is so dark because I don't want him to see me blushing again. I wish I had the kind of skin that could conceal embarrassment instead of blooming out in bright pink for all the world to see.

"Why am I here?" I rattle the handcuff impatiently. I want to add *and why am I naked?* But I don't want to draw attention to this vulnerability even though I know he knows about it because he's probably the one who took my clothes off.

I want to beg him to let me go, but I'm not quite there yet. I don't want to be so pathetic so quickly—especially since it's still hard for me to believe this has happened. And there's a part of me still convinced he wouldn't hurt me because of Livia even though I'm now not sure if he'd hurt Livia.

But wouldn't he? Maybe he's a secret serial killer. I saw a six-part series on TV about killers who lived normal lives and nobody suspected until they had a big body count and were in handcuffs in a courtroom with cold dead-eyed stares which nobody seemed to notice before that exact moment. Their wives all thought they were wonderful.

After that I went down an internet rabbit trail about it and couldn't sleep properly for a month. It also didn't do my dating life any favors. On the one hand I was afraid I might date a serial killer, and on the other I was afraid I might be the girl who gets serial-killed while the clueless wife sits at home thinking he's amazing. So maybe Soren is that kind of crazy.

He sighs. "As I said, you're unfortunately the sacrifice. You see, I have a... what do you girls call it? A frenemy? Apparently some things I said caused some problems for him, and he believes I owe him. He's threatened to tell the world the truth about my unconventional marriage. This would also spill out onto Dayne and Griffin. And of course it would affect Livia. So you are the sacrifice that stops all that unpleasantness and keeps all our stock prices up."

He keeps saying that word: *sacrifice*. And I don't quite know what it means, but I know it can't be good.

He's quiet for a long time.

"You need to let me go," I say. My voice is less strong than I'd like. "Livia will never forgive you if you hurt me." Is he going to hurt me? I'm so confused about what's going on. My head still hurts and feels weird from the drugs so I hear the words he's saying but most of them make no sense to me at least not enough for any deep thinking or analyzing.

"You're going to stay here and be a good girl for Colin."

"W-who's Colin?"

Soren just smiles. "The man who now owns you."

Twin feelings of terror and arousal flood my system at these words because it's not like I can just dismantle my entire sexual circuitry just because I'm an actual captive now. My responses are completely involuntary.

"A-and if I don't?"

"You will."

I wonder suddenly if he'll blackmail me about what I now think of as The Incident. About ten years ago, Livia and I went to Panama City for Spring Break. She was almost raped but somehow managed to kill the guy. In her struggle, she grabbed a large piece of jagged broken glass and swiped out, severing the artery in his neck. He bled out in seconds.

She called me instead of the cops because she was afraid no one would believe her since a lot of people had seen her with him at a party earlier that night. He was very popular. Nobody ever believes the hot popular guy could be a rapist —or that any woman would ever need to kill him in self defense. Because of course no woman could really say no to him. We may have come a long way, but women still aren't assumed to have agency with a man if he's well-liked, looks amazing, and has money. And that power combo? The triple threat? Forget about it. You flirt with that guy and you fuck him because nobody will believe your accusations when he crosses the line later anyway.

I helped Livia get rid of the body that night. It's the leverage Soren used to get her to marry him, and part of me is afraid he'll use that same leverage now for whatever this is.

But I know he won't because Soren doesn't bluff. He won't let Livia go to prison now that he has her securely tied to him. It's probably why he drugged and kidnapped me. It's not like he needs blackmail to get his way this time. I'm already captured.

Soren stands and moves closer to the bed. He stares down at me and strokes the side of my cheek. He seems like he might say something else. But instead he turns and leaves, closing the door softly behind him. I feel suddenly a bit like a pet that's been sadly left at the pound because a family member is allergic.

"Soren! Don't leave me here! Please..." I'm crying now. He's really leaving me in this strange house with some man he's just *given me to* as if he has that right. I was never his to give. But laws and rules don't matter to Soren Kingston. He's his own law.

# 3

## MACY

When I wake this time the room is completely dark, the sun having long set. I have no idea what time it is. I don't even remember falling asleep again, but I must have cried myself to sleep. And now I'm hungry. I'm hungry, I have to pee, and I'm tied naked to a bed, *the sacrifice* to someone I've never met. My overactive imagination visualizes a huge terrifying beast will come to devour me when some distant clock strikes midnight.

"Soren?" I call, because I need to believe Soren is still here, that he hasn't left me alone here with... what was the guy's name? I can't remember. I'm only just now feeling semi-normal from the earlier drugging. I don't know why I hope Soren is still here except that he's the devil I know. And now that I'm thinking more clearly I hope I can reason with him somehow. Surely he can give this man something besides me.

Even if Soren were still here, he wouldn't hear me. I didn't call out loudly enough. And yet, after a few short minutes, the bedroom door opens letting light spill in from the hallway. The light falls over me on the bed, and I squint against it. I scramble to sit up, hissing as the handcuff digs into my wrist. I use my free hand to secure the white sheet over my body, preserving my modesty as well as I can.

"S-Soren?"

"Soren went home." The voice is male, low, and dark. If possible, he sounds even more ruthless than Soren, and my body reacts immediately. I haven't even seen this guy. Just three small words, and my body is excited. It clearly has no sense of self-preservation. I had thought this reaction was exclusive to Soren, but no, it's just men *like* Soren. With my body obviously against my survival, it's a miracle I haven't already ended up dead in a ditch somewhere.

Like Soren, this man has an overpowering ruthless energy that I can feel heavy on the air around me. It makes every nerve ending light up in response with the desire to be consumed and ripped apart by this new storm.

I can feel it in the air. He is darkness. I am light. He is guilty. I am innocent. He is war. I am love.

I'm sick. There probably isn't even a diagnosis for what's wrong with me.

I wish I could control my body's reaction. There are just some things that set me off in this primal animal way. Intellectually I know this man may really hurt me. Or he may be gross. Or he may be any number of horrible things, but even so, I'm wet.

He's cast in too much shadow for me to see his face, which calls back my fantasy from this morning, something else I definitely don't need to be thinking about right now. I'm not an idiot. I know I'm in real trouble here, and that this isn't some fantasy that's come to life. But I feel pulled into him as though the storm can provide me shelter.

All I can see are his shiny expensive shoes and his suit. I can't tell what color it is, but it's dark. Black or Navy.

He steps fully into the room, leaving the door open, then

slips further into the shadows so that he feels more like a ghostly presence than a real person. But even if I hadn't seen his silhouette pass through, I would feel him. That's how loud his presence is.

"Do you know why you're here?" he finally says.

"N-no."

But I think I do. I mean I'm given to some guy as payment for some debt, and I'm naked. It's not exactly an unsolvable riddle. And it makes my arousal right now so inappropriate. I don't even know if I'll fight him. I don't know if I can. Not because I'll lose—which I know I will—but because I've been starved of male touch well past a point that's normal, and I need... I can't let my mind finish that thought. I will *not* finish that thought. What I need is a straitjacket and a room with soft walls so I can't hurt myself.

It occurs to me that I never felt in a big hurry for Will to touch me. Not once did my body remind me how starved it was for the sexual act while Will was taking me out on dates as a prelude to our sham of a wedding. And here this man—whose face I haven't even seen—speaks three uninspiring words to me, and I have to fight to keep my legs closed.

The stranger sighs. "What did Soren tell you about your situation?"

"H-he said I was a sacrifice. S-so his stock prices don't fall." I've just remembered that last part, and it enrages me enough to quiet my body's insistent whining for a moment.

The man chuckles at this. "And do you know what that means? That you're a sacrifice?"

I shake my head. I perversely seem to need him to spell out every tiny detail of my situation as though it's just another fantasy I'll touch myself to later instead of my actual harrowing real life fate.

"It means you now exist at my pleasure and for my pleasure. It means I'm going to take your innocence and keep you as my toy."

"I-I'm supposed to be getting married," I blurt out inanely. This is what I mean about socially awkward. Who says that in this situation? Like he cares about my wedding plans.

"Oh really? And when will that be?"

"In six months. I-in March."

"Well maybe I'll be tired of you by then and I can give you back to him well broken in. I'm sure your new husband will thank me for all that I'll teach you."

I start crying then, my reality finally eclipsing my body's stupid response to this man. "Please, I-I need to use the bathroom." I meant to beg him to let me go home, but my physical need to pee far outranks the larger need to get out of this house and escape whatever this stranger has planned for me. I still can't remember his name.

I flinch when he moves closer. The darkness cloaks him as though he's the grim reaper himself. He unlocks the cuff then points to a door behind me. "The bathroom's there."

I hesitate, remembering my nudity and try to figure out how to navigate this situation. Finally I tug at the sheet to free it from the rest of the bed and wrap it completely around myself, careful not to reveal anything. He makes no comment about this. We both know it's a pointless delay.

I shut and lock the door behind me before turning the bathroom light on. It's much larger than I expected for a bathroom connected to what seemed to me to be a guest bedroom. It's definitely not his room. I don't know why I'm so sure about this, but I am. The bathroom is black and white, both simple and elegant and also kind of old-fashioned somehow. That's when I realize this is a very old house and these are the original faucets.

After using the facilities, I test the latch on the window.

Locked. But I realize to my dismay that we're not on the first floor anyway. It doesn't even feel like the second, we're so high up. Does his house have three floors? Who has three floors?

I pace back and forth for several minutes trying to figure out what to do next. I contemplate just staying in here forever, but I'm sure he can get in if he really wants to. I fight with myself for several more minutes before slowly unlocking the door. I don't bother turning the bathroom light off, but he still manages to stay out of the path of light even with another strip of it now flooding the room.

I'm beginning to think he doesn't want me to see him at all. Does he have some sort of disfiguring scar or is it to protect his identity? If I see him will he not ever let me go? Does he really plan to let me go? He implied he might.

This has me wondering if I don't please him will he let me go sooner, or will he do something worse?

He sits in a chair in the far corner, legs spread, relaxed. At least he looks relaxed. He doesn't *feel* relaxed to me. And I'm not sure where I've gotten these extra senses from all of a sudden, but I can feel him even from across the room in a way I've never felt another person's presence.

"Drop the sheet. I want to look at Soren's offering, to make sure I approve and can clear his debt."

From the way Soren spoke the debt wasn't even monetary, not really. Soren just did something that inconvenienced this guy in some way. Somehow this feels even worse for me.

His order makes me clutch the sheet tighter. My gaze goes to the open bedroom door.

"Don't even think about it. I run five miles a day. I'm much faster than you, and I don't want to have to punish you your first night."

I let out a hysterical and inappropriate laugh. I have zero

control of my weird emotional reactions right now. The laugh is because I can't believe he really thinks I'm going to just obediently drop the sheet. I haven't even seen this man's face yet, and he wants to see everything from me?

My gaze darts around the room, finally landing on a vase of flowers on the night table nearest to me. This is when I realize that while I was sleeping someone came in and changed out the flowers. Is this guy a florist? Where is he getting all these fresh flowers?

This new vase isn't glass. It's silver and looks very heavy. Before I can think it through or let him figure out what I'm planning, I pick it up and hurl it at him. Without waiting to see how it lands, I rush out the door and down the hallway, his snarled curses ringing in my ears. I go down two flights of stairs and out the front door, clutching the sheet to me.

As soon as the door to the outside world opens, an ear-splitting siren starts to blare. I have to stop a moment to gather the sheet so it doesn't drag and cause me to trip. Then I take off at a full run, my bare feet landing softly against the manicured lawn. I glance back once at the enormous foreboding estate, then continue on.

I'm grateful when the open space finally ends in a thickly wooded area. I have to go slower in the woods because there are so many trees, and the ground isn't as soft, but at least I have cover to hide in. Finally, out of breath and exhausted, I slow my pace to walking.

I don't think he's even chasing me. The sirens have stopped blaring, but he hasn't shouted after me. I haven't heard any footsteps running. Maybe he decided it wasn't worth it to chase me down. Maybe I knocked him out cold with the vase?

It's only now that I've slowed down that I realize my feet and legs and arms are covered in small cuts from branches, sticks, and rocks. And now that it doesn't seem like anyone is chasing me my fear shifts to the dark woods and what might be lurking out here. Snakes? Bears? Wolves? Hell, I don't know. I don't know how far out we are or what wildlife may be present.

It's the dark moon so I can barely even see my hand in front of my face. And it's unseasonably cold for a late September night. I'm cold, hungry, bleeding, lost. I don't know what to do or where to go. For all I know this is the actual forest and it could go on for miles and miles like this. I could starve out here or freeze to death.

I don't know what else to do but sit on the dirty ground and cry and hope for the sun to rise.

"MA'AM? I'm officer Duke. Are you all right?"

I squint up at a flashlight. I don't know how long I've been sitting out here, and I'm starting to worry about hypothermia.

"I-I need help. Please... someone kidnapped me." I realize suddenly that he's not alone. There are a couple other officers with him. They help me to stand, and then one of them picks me up to carry me back the way they came.

The one who spoke to me pulls out a cell phone and dials a number. "Colin, we've got her. We're bringing her back to the house."

Colin. That's his name.

"What? No! You can't take me back to him. He kidnapped me. He's holding me prisoner!" I struggle in the arms of the man carrying me, but his grip is firm. Why are the police taking me back to him?

Maybe I misunderstood. Maybe he didn't say he was a police officer. Maybe Colin has private security on the house and sent them after me. It doesn't take very long to get back, which makes me realize I must have been mostly going in circles when I was in the woods.

Once we reach light, I see two police squad cars in the driveway. So no, they aren't private security. The actual police are taking me back to my captor as if this is all normal and okay. I've stopped struggling because there's no point, and I'm so grateful to be back inside the warm house. The immediate problem of freezing at least has been solved.

The officer carrying me takes me down a long hallway on the main floor and into what looks like a library. The walls are dark rich mahogany, and there's a large fireplace with a healthy crackling fire. The heat coming off it feels like life itself. The officer puts me on the ground in front of the fire. From my vantage point I can only see Colin's black shoes and suit pants.

"Thank you for retrieving her. I'll wire you some money in the morning."

The police don't say anything. They just turn and leave, shutting the library doors behind them.

"I assume that's the last time you'll run from me now that you understand how pointless it is," Colin says.

I look up to find furious icy blue eyes on me as I'm confronted with the face of my captor for the first time. Aside from the rage coming off him, he's beautiful. Tall, maybe six foot three, well built, chiseled jaw, full lips, blonde, tan. He looks like he stepped out of a magazine spread for sailboat enthusiasts. I swallow hard when I realize he's not wearing a shirt. My gaze is drawn to a large angry bruise on his chest near his shoulder. It looks fresh. From the vase I threw? Oops.

He leaves the room without another word. A few minutes later the door opens again and it's another man, a bit older than Colin. I flinch and shrink back, but then I spot what he's carrying: a tray with soup on it.

The man places the tray on the ground beside me. "You need to eat something, ma'am." He has a crisp formal British accent.

This is the most I ever remember being called ma'am in my life. He leaves me alone, and I eat the soup. It's really more of a hearty beef stew than a soup, and it didn't come out of a can. I wonder if he started making it as soon as I ran out the front door or if they just happened to have it already made. Talk about anticipating people's needs. Is this guy the butler?

He's too good-looking to be a butler. And he doesn't look like a bodyguard, though he does seem stronger than your average butler—not that I would know—all I know about butlers comes from TV and movies. I'm mostly familiar with all the versions of Batman's butler. So that's probably not a huge window into reality I can count on.

When the food's gone, I move closer to the fire. My feet are finally warmer. I was afraid to look at them, for fear I'd see signs of frost bite, but they're normal color and the feeling is coming back. My cuts and scrapes are worse than I thought, but before I can start to worry about infection, the library door opens again.

I jump at the intrusion, but it's only the man who brought me food. "Ma'am, I've drawn you a bath."

I gawk at him for a moment before I can finally form words. "I-I need to get out of here. I need to go home. He's keeping me prisoner. Please, you have to help me."

Surely Colin doesn't own the entire police department. It's probably just the officers that came out tonight. I could still report him and get free and go back to my life. And planning my tragic wedding to a man I don't want?

Suddenly that seems a lot better than this. Safe. Boring. I find I'm ready now to succumb to safe and boring.

He shakes his head. "You belong to Mr. Black now. Your life will be easier if you accept this."

I wonder briefly if I hit my head and I'm dreaming. Is everyone around my captor a brainwashed drone? How much is he paying them? Does he have blackmail on them all? I can't understand what would motivate police officers and butlers to cover for this guy's crimes and enable him in carrying them out so easily.

"H-has he done this before?"

"Done what, Ma'am?"

"Kidnapped a woman."

He laughs at this. "Oh no. Mr. Black didn't kidnap you. He accepted you as payment for a debt from Mr. Kingston." He says all this as if I don't know this story and as if it's not completely insane no matter how he phrases it or how many times I hear it.

"Okay, has he ever accepted... *payment* of this nature for anything before? And if so, what happened to those women?" They're probably buried somewhere on his vast property. I shudder at that thought.

"His previous toys came to him of their own volition. They were compensated well for their time."

I bet they were.

I want to throw the empty soup bowl at this man. I'm so close to going off on a tirade about how evil happens when people just follow orders, as clearly everyone in Colin's life does without question or complaint. If he thinks I'm going to be one of his little order followers, he's miscalculated.

I decide now that I don't care about his fucking money or his looks or whatever it is about him that makes my body want to open and welcome him inside. I'm not going to be one of these morons falling at his feet. I won't make this easy on him.

"Do you know both he and Soren referred to me as a *sacrifice*? Like some offering on an altar. How the hell do you sleep at night?"

Before the butler can answer my accusations, the door opens again and Colin strides into the room, his hard gaze locked on mine. I'm sure he heard me from out in the hallway and I wonder how much of the conversation he listened in on before he decided to interrupt.

"That'll be all, Jeffrey. I'll take it from here."

"Of course, Sir."

Then Colin's obedient mindless robot drone leaves me alone with him.

"You can't keep me here like this." It's probably the stupidest thing I could say in this moment. My indignance borders on cartoonish.

"Oh? All evidence points to the contrary." He sounds bored.

"C-can I call Livia?" I know this is a stupid question to ask but it still came right out of my mouth.

She'll be worried sick. And then there's Will. And my job. I'm a research librarian. I help academics at the university find the things they need for their various papers and studies. Professor McKracken and I have been on an art history research deep dive for the past three weeks, so I will be missed.

"It's after one in the morning," he says.

"Tomorrow then. She'll worry. Don't prisoners get one phone call?"

He laughs. "Oh, Macy, you're not a prisoner. You're a sacrifice, remember? A gift to appease my wrath."

This wrath still simmers in his gaze as he studies me,

and I find myself shivering once again, though not from the cold.

I scramble backwards when he approaches, but he's too fast. He picks me up and carries me out of the room and up to the second floor. I'm trying hard not to marvel at the fact that he can carry me this far and up stairs without even getting winded.

We go down the long darkened hallway into an expansive masculine room which I'm sure is his, and then through to an equally impressive bathroom.

Steam still rises up off the water in the huge tub. Jeffrey must have run it on scalding hot. Colin sets me down on my feet, and I hiss in pain and grip the edge of the counter.

"Sit," he orders, pointing to the wide tile ledge of the tub.

I sit, relieved to not be standing on the cuts and bruises I suffered in the woods.

"Now, let's try again. Drop the sheet." The order comes out more insistent than it did earlier in the guest room.

I shake my head furiously, gripping the dirty ripped sheet tight against my body. Tears begin moving down my cheeks again. "Please... N-no one's ever seen..."

His eyes widen as he realizes what I'm trying to convey to him, that no one... at least no one adult and male has ever seen me naked. He covers his shock quickly. "Soren saw. He's the one who undressed you and put you in bed."

My entire body flushes at this, even though I suspected it was probably Soren who took my clothing.

He watches me for another moment then says, "When I return you will be naked in that water or else."

I watch as he turns on his heel and leaves, slamming the door behind him.

# 4

## COLIN

As soon as I'm out of the bathroom, I lean against the door, my fists clenching and unclenching at my sides. It's involuntary. I'm not going to fucking hit her or anything—at least not with a fist. She isn't a man. Men get punched, women get spanked. Or paddled. Or cropped. Or caned. I'm not a complete monster.

I pick up the phone on my nightstand. It doesn't dial out. I've long given up my landline for the ease and convenience of my cell. The phone is wired up as an intercom system to dial downstairs now. Jeffrey picks up on the third ring.

"Yes, Sir?"

"I need some ointment and bandages to tend to the girl's injuries."

"I'll bring them up right away."

Jeffrey has been with me for the last ten years. He's a man of few words, no questions, and no judgment. He's seen the dirtiest of my dealings both in blood and in sex, and he hasn't once flinched. Frankly that makes me wonder about him, but there was nothing concerning in his background check.

Though if he knew what he was doing, that could have been scrubbed easily enough.

I run a Fortune 500 company, but on a certain level it's become more of a criminal enterprise. Half the business I do these days is off the books. I've somehow gotten into shit in the past five years that would shock the mob. And I've started behaving like a mob boss in how I deal with my problems. More than one person has conveniently disappeared after threatening me with multi-million dollar lawsuits. I just don't like threats. They bother me. Especially threats that involve me having less money.

It's definitely not how my father handled the business, but I've become addicted to the power of it all and the feeling of invincibility. I'm either a sociopath or an adrenaline junkie, possibly some combination of both. I've taken things many steps farther than my father ever did, both by dealing with my problems in unconventional and illegal ways, and by my sexual habits which run equally dark.

If Soren were any other person in the world, his decision to fuck with my business dealings—however inadvertent—would have cost him his life. Instead, I decided to be more petty and less lethal. Besides, I try not to shit where I eat, and Soren isn't far removed enough from me to keep suspicion at bay if he turned up missing. I'm not a crazed psychopath with no self-control after all.

If he disappeared and it came back on me, well, that would probably revoke my membership at the club in Costa Rica, not to mention the risk of prison. It's not Soren's club, but Soren shares his wife with the man who owns it. So killing him was never anything more than a passing fantasy.

I'd be lying if I said I wasn't concerned with my own thirst for other people's blood and the guilt that never materializes over that reality. I sometimes wonder if there is a *me* inside this hollow shell at all. I know I'm not normal inside, but maybe I just have the balls to do what other men only fantasize about.

Maybe the problem is that I think life is a game. I've always thought this way. There's a sort of unreal quality about everything in the world to me, and I often think of others as mere characters in a virtual world—characters in my own playground, as if they exist only to move my story forward—as if they don't have their own personalities or desires; it's mere window-dressing, the shallow backstory of extras.

But hey, maybe that's what happened. Maybe technology advanced to the point that I really am playing a game set inside an earlier timeline. Yes, I know how that sounds. I know what it says about me. Crazy? Narcissist? I don't know. But I'm not right inside. I know that much. And isn't admitting you have a problem the first step?

Shouldn't I get some sort of pin or ribbon for this?

And here I am, crossing yet another line. Initially I'd thought to get Soren to loan his blushing new bride to me, but he came up with something better... *something sweet, that I can keep forever... with conditions.*

That something sweet is of course the beautiful and innocent Macy Laine. The condition Soren gave me was that I had to secure her future. Legally. I had to marry her. From his twisted perspective this somehow protects her and alleviates his guilt because she'll be provided for in a lifestyle she could have only dreamed about before. From my perspective it just seals her doom. Not all money is good money. And I am most definitely *not* good money.

He and I negotiated because I have no interest in getting entangled in a marriage with the state, being beholden to their arbitrary whims and rules of how things will go in my relationship and how they will go should that relationship ever end—not that it would ever end without my say so.

I don't understand why anyone would make a marriage contract with someone that they can't even dictate the terms of. So I had my attorneys draw up a *private* business contract which Soren read and approved.

By this point I'd already mostly given up my personal vendetta against him, solely focused on claiming this new tempting prize and starting this new game, this new diversion. Besides, a wife looks good to the stockholders. If I'm going to have a body count, I need to look as normal and respectable on the outside as possible. And nobody will make me look more normal and respectable than Macy.

This girl is so innocent and sweet, she doesn't even have so much as a traffic ticket on her record. I couldn't resist the urge to taunt her, to suggest that I might deflower her, use her, train her to all my dark and twisted desires, then return her to the man she's meant to marry. Of course that was a lie. She's mine.

I'm still not entirely sure why I accepted Soren's conditions. I didn't have to. I'm the one with the power here. I could have done as I'd threatened and outed his poly relationship to the world. But when I saw her and found out just how untouched she is, I was too greedy to fight him on his terms. I was all too eager at the prospect of keeping her, of *creating her* from the very beginning.

I don't have an unnatural attraction to purity for the sake of it. It's just that she has no bad training to undo. She's had no shitty lovers. She's picked up no bad habits. She's not jaded. She's not bored. Everything is new and exciting and terrifying, just the way I like it with a girl. And it gets tiresome to pay for the reactions that will all flow freely and naturally out of Macy.

When Soren brought her here, I wanted him to undress her and put her in the bed so I could take my time unveiling her. That didn't turn out quite as expected. I press my fingertips against the bruise where the vase hit me. Fucking redheads, man. Even the sweet ones are lethal. If she'd hit me a little higher up and to the left she could have knocked me unconscious. I do everything in my power to ignore the twinge of fear at what might have happened to her out in the woods if I'd been unconscious for any length of time. It's an uncomfortable and unfamiliar feeling, fear. I wasn't even sure I could feel such a thing, and I'm torn between whether or not I should punish her for introducing me to this new unsettling emotion.

There's a curt knock on my door.

"Come in."

Jeffrey enters the room with the bandages and ointment I requested. We keep all that stuff downstairs in the servant's quarters, but I should probably keep a supply in my bathroom as well.

He drops everything on the bed and leaves. I'm surprised he hasn't said anything about Macy and my plans for her. He knows how innocent the girl is.

When I re-enter the bathroom she's in the tub, crying quietly. The water has gone a very pale pink from her blood. It isn't that any one wound is particularly dangerous, it's that there are so many of them. Three or four marks on each of her legs and her arms. And I'm sure there are some on the bottoms of her feet.

I'm not sure if she's crying about the pain of the water on those cuts or the hopelessness of her fate with me. She should save her tears for me. The cuts will fade. I wish I was the kind of man who could say these tears move me, stir some kind of guilt in me, make me feel like a monster craving redemption. But they don't. They just make me want to take her until her tears turn to moans and she surrenders to the heights of pleasure I'll take her to.

She's so completely perfect.

"Tears only excite me, so you should probably find a way to stop them."

She glances up startled, and it takes all my self control not to lean forward and lick the tears off her cheeks like some wild animal.

# 5

## MACY

I glance up to find his erection pressing against his pants. I would say it's terrifyingly large but I don't have a lot to compare it with. I'm not sure what's normal. He's not kidding about the tears exciting him, though this man doesn't seem like the practical joker type.

I turn away and try to stop crying like he suggested, but I can't. I've managed to quiet the tears, but they continue to roll down my cheeks no matter how strongly I will them away. I think I've cried more in the past few hours than I have for my entire life up until this point.

In general I don't cry a lot. Today is the most I've cried in years between the crying on the phone with Livia this morning and now. That feels so far away. Was that really just this morning? And the dress shopping? Was that truly this afternoon?

If I'd thought I didn't have enough normal emotions, I'm strangely relieved to know that's untrue. I have plenty of emotions. I'd just never had much to cry about before now. I should feel grateful for that, but even though I'm not on speaking terms with my family, I'm realizing how otherwise sheltered I've been from the world and how little real loss I've suffered. And now to have everything stolen from me in a moment is just too much.

My safety, my freedom, my apartment, my job at the university, my best friend, my stupid wedding to an *enough* man that I don't love. Even that last part feels like a loss because I'm not sure Colin will ever let me go, then I'll never have *any* wedding. I may not even get a funeral.

I stare at the blood tinged water. "Are you really going to let me go... w-when you're finished with me?" I don't know how long that will be. A few nights? A few weeks? Months?

I jump when his mouth is suddenly at my ear. "Never," he growls. It's a possessive claiming sound that no man has ever directed toward me before. And as badly as I want to say it is, not all of my shiver is from fear.

I turn to him as he pulls away and straightens. "B-but I thought you said..."

"And what? You're shocked that a man who would keep you captive and train you to be his obedient toy would tell you a lie? Really, Macy? Surely you aren't that naive."

I take a deep shuddering breath. "A-are you going to kill me?" *Shut up, Macy. Why even ask this question? What good could possibly come of it?*

He chuckles at this like the ending of my life is a hilarious concept. "I think we've already established that I'm an unreliable narrator so even if I promise to spare you, do you think you should believe me?"

I can't bring myself to look at his face again, but I can't stop looking at the bruise on his shoulder.

He notices and says, "Don't worry, I won't punish you tonight. You didn't leave me much canvas to play with, now did you?"

He gestures to my injuries, and the hiccuping sobs start again. I should have just kept moving in the woods. With each passing second the thought of being ripped apart by a wolf or a bear feels like a better ending than this sociopath and whatever cruelly creative torture he might devise.

I flinch when he sits on the edge of the tub, and then he's stroking the side of my throat, his intense gaze locked on mine. Inexplicably my tears stop. One second they're flowing down my cheeks in steady streams, and the next, they just... stop. I take a deep breath. Everything inside me goes still. It isn't prey stillness. It's not the fear I felt half a second ago and know I should still feel.

Against every rational instinct, I find his touch calming. This is somehow more shameful to me than my arousal, that I would be stupid enough to let down my guard with this monster, that I would allow the person who created this terror to soothe it away with a gentle touch.

It takes every ounce of concentration and self control not to lean into his large warm hand like a cat seeking affection. I won't let myself seek affection from this man. If I do I can kiss goodbye the thought that I could ever be normal in any way. The number of things wrong with my brain and my body only climb higher with each passing second in Colin's presence.

"Look at me," he says. His hand hasn't stopped stroking the side of my neck. It's a slow, gentle repetitive movement. Calming. Hypnotic.

I realize suddenly I've been zoning out, staring at the water. And somehow in the intensity of his presence I've forgotten my nudity. I look up to find cold blue eyes burning through me. That's what it seems like. He is cold, but somehow I still feel so warm. His touch, his gaze, they ignite something inside me that spreads out in a fluttery warmth, culminating in what I'm sure is wet heat between my legs, and I've never been more grateful to be shielded by the water.

He may be able to see me, but my other secrets are safe, at least for the moment. But he isn't assessing my body. His eyes don't leave mine. He's making decisions and calculations about my soul.

After a moment, a choice is made and he leans closer. My breathing stops as he licks the wetness off the side of my cheek. And this just makes me start crying again. This act somehow breaks the peace and strange calm. It feels too *serial killer* to me, and I'm once again worried at the possible new brevity of my life.

"I fucking love these tears," he growls against my cheek. He pulls one of my hands from the water and places my wet hand on his erection as if I needed proof.

"Please don't hurt me." It comes out a whisper, but I know he hears me.

He pulls back, and his eyes meet mine. I've never felt so many feelings in one moment before. I don't even have names for categories to put them all in, which disturbs me. I've always been so organized. I've always been able to know what everything is and where to put it. But I don't know where to put anything now because there's just too many feelings I don't understand. And too many fears I can't give voice to.

Fears I'm crazy. Fears he'll kill me. Fears he won't and I'll become something even more abnormal because everything about this moment and my reaction to it is so very wrong.

He stands abruptly, dumping my hand from his lap. He doesn't look at me when he speaks. "Clean yourself up then come back out to the bedroom. No towel. Just come to me..." His heated hungry gaze sweeps over me. "... like this. You have fifteen minutes."

His shoes click decisively across the tile floor, and then I'm alone in the bathroom with his orders ringing in my ears. It may as well be fifteen minutes left to live from the way he said those words. I want to ask how the hell I'll know if I'm late, but then I notice a clock on the countertop sitting between the two sinks.

Now that the room is so quiet and he's left me alone again, I can hear the ticking. It's so loud I don't know how I could have blocked the sound out before. All I want right now is to feel safe. I want to go back to that insane moment where somehow his hand at the side of my throat gave me the feeling that everything was going to be okay, that he would *make* it okay.

I uselessly start crying again, but I do what he said and get cleaned up. I use every single second that clock affords me trying to live in the eternal now just to stretch it out as long as possible, to savor each second of pretend safety I've been afforded.

Finally I get out of the tub and dry off.

I notice a robe hanging on a hook on the wall. I want to put it on, but I'm afraid of what will happen if I disobey him. And I know modesty is a stupid thing to try to preserve or reclaim in these circumstances. I wish I had that siren thing. Seduction feels like the one way to reclaim power or at least possibly save my own life. When he realizes I don't have that siren thing, it's over. The novelty of my innocence won't hold his interest once he realizes just how boring I truly am.

"You're one minute late," he says when I step out into the bedroom.

"I-I'm sorry." I look at the ground because I can't meet his sharp gaze anymore, and I need to pretend he's not looking at me.

He prowls around me in a slow methodical way. "Not yet, but you will be."

"Please... I'm sorry. Please," I whimper. The promise that I *will be* sorry has stolen my ability to think clear thoughts or take oxygen from the air around me.

"Master," he says. "I own you. So you will call me Master."

"Master," I hear myself say like his obedient sex robot. This word is a trigger—like in those movies where someone has been programmed by the government to be a killing machine, but they don't know it. They're just going about their lives, then one day the phone rings, and the voice on the other side says the trigger word and they go into kill mode.

That's what the word *Master* does to me. Except instead of kill mode it sends me into extreme sexual excitement mode. It's just been a part of my sexual fantasies for too long. Too many orgasms have come along with that word. The trigger is too deep, too strong. I'll never be able to deactivate it.

And now this evil crazy guy is using the trigger, and just like that, my desire belongs to him. I'm not suddenly unafraid of who he might be and what he might do to me. It's just that my body is no longer capable of not reacting to this word. I kind of knew a part of me was already lost. He's too attractive. It's that, along with his ruthless chaotic storm energy and the undercurrents that were in the air long before this moment of full admission of exactly what he is to me.

But I'd held out a small hope that I could push through all that and *not* react like this to my captor—or at least regain control of myself with time. Now all I want to do is kneel. I just want to give in, let him take me down this dark road, surrender to it and let the fantasies be real even if just for a little while.

I flinch when he takes a step closer. He invades my personal space and then he's touching me again, stroking the side of my throat, and I melt into him just as I did the last time he touched me. I'm so fucked up. I have no idea how I've managed to go about life pretending to be normal. There's nothing normal about me. It would be different if this were someone I trusted, and we were playing a game. But we aren't, and I don't. I could never trust someone like this. A man with soulless ice where his eyes should be. A man who thinks you can own a person and is just fine with it.

"You're going to be a very good girl for me, aren't you, Macy?" he says as his hand moves up to stroke my cheek.

A fluttery wave moves through my stomach.

"Y-yes, Master."

I look away from the satisfied smirk on his face, back to the ground, the only safe thing to look at.

"Good girl. Go lie down on the bed."

I want to turn and run again, but I already know how futile that is. I wonder how many punishments are coming. I was late. I threw a vase at him. I ran away.

Is he going to take my virginity right here and now? I'm pretty sure it will hurt. I've been tempted to try to break the barrier myself with a sex toy, but I lost my nerve every time I thought about doing it because I really have next to no tolerance for pain, which makes my fantasies even more insane.

Maybe if I could have just done that, no one ever would have had to know I'd never had sex, and I could have maybe found someone by now. Because it wouldn't be weird; it wouldn't push the good men away. And if I'd done that and found someone, surely I wouldn't be here now.

I can't believe I've already spiraled to a point of madness where I've convinced myself if I'd had the nerve to masturbate with a dildo years ago I would somehow be safe from Colin.

"Now, Macy."

I jump at his hot breath in my ear. He presses a kiss

against the side of my throat, and this horrifying sound of longing slips past my lips before I can stop it.

"On your stomach," he says as I go to the bed.

"But... why?" Is he going to take me from behind?

Why can't I just admit to myself I want this man to touch me? Who cares if he's evil and had me kidnapped? I need to be touched. I just want all the thoughts in my head to stop for once. Can't I stop analyzing for one second? Can't I stop morally judging myself? It's not like this is my fault. It's not like I self-kidnapped.

"Now," he repeats quietly.

I lie down on the bed not sure if I feel more or less exposed than I would if I were lying on my back. But he doesn't take off his clothes or touch me in any inappropriate way. And I'm just now realizing that when he was touching my throat and the side of my cheek just now, his hand only needed to slide down a few inches to touch my breasts, but he didn't. What does that mean?

Is it me? Is there something wrong with me? Why does every man show so much restraint with me?

I need him to do whatever he's going to do so I can decide how I feel about it. I can't take this anticipation anymore. And my brain is freaking out not being allowed to put things into categories.

Instead, he rubs a cool gel into the cuts on the backs of my legs. I'd forgotten I even had them. The pain had dulled to a vague sort of background throb. I lie still as he takes his time taping gauze down over the cuts. Then he takes care of the bottoms of my feet and the backs of my arms.

"Roll over," he says when he's finished.

I roll over to my back, and he repeats this process with the cuts on the front of my body. He's lost in concentration as he does this. His heated gaze occasionally travels slowly up my body, to my eyes, and then back down again. I feel like a tiny flying insect trapped in a spider's web, and he's taking his time wrapping me up for his later consumption.

Colin doesn't say anything else. When he's finished, he puts everything back inside the first aid kit, then stands and covers me with the blankets.

"Go to sleep."

He turns off the light and leaves the room, shutting the door behind him. I hear a key turn in the lock and realize he's locked me in for the night. I lay in the dark, feeling my heartbeat thudding against my chest as it tries to slow back down to a normal rhythm. I didn't realize how scared I was until he left me alone for the night.

And now I'm even more on edge because I can't understand why he's doing what he's doing. I don't mean the kidnapping and enslaving part. I don't need a special explanation for that. Some people are just bad. I mean the *not* touching me part. The not fucking me or hurting me part.

I mean, I threw a really heavy vase at him. He's got a dark purple bruise. I ran away. And he hasn't missed a beat, as if he expected all of these reactions and had already made allowances for them—like he'd already decided to forgive me for them.

He doesn't return, and I realize just how exhausted I am. I'm just going to close my eyes for a minute.

When I open my eyes again, sun streams through the windows. The digital clock on the nightstand says it's eleven thirty. I bolt up in bed as I remember where I am. I'm still alone in the bed. But where did Colin sleep?

I look at the empty space beside me. The other side of the bed is clearly slept in, and when I press my hand against the sheets, they're still warm from his body. Realization that he slept here—with me—brings with it a cold chill. He must have come back to bed after I'd fallen asleep.

How did I sleep through the night with him beside me?

Why didn't I wake up? Did he touch me? I'm sure I would have woken if he had. But then I'm sure I *should* have woken if he'd come back into the room at all, which he clearly did.

Did he lie next to me and watch me sleep like some creepy weirdo? Did he pull me against his body? Was he naked, too?

Before I can go deeper down the rabbit hole of this sinister sleeping situation, the phone rings. I just stare at it. But it rings and rings. It's a landline. Who even has landlines anymore? And there apparently isn't a voice mailbox set up because it just *keeps* ringing.

Finally I pick up the receiver just to make the noise stop. "H-hello?"

"Come down for breakfast," Colin says. Then the line goes dead.

# 6

## COLIN

I pace in the bright airy kitchen waiting for her. Jeffrey has prepared an elaborate brunch with more options than she's probably used to. I barely slept last night, yet somehow she slept soundly even though I'd pulled her against my body, my arm wrapped around her to prevent escape—like if I didn't keep touching her she'd disappear.

I have no idea how she slept through it except that it was late and she was exhausted from all the fear and running and being out in the cold woods. Maybe she's just one of those people who could sleep through a hurricane once she's worn out enough.

No woman has ever begged me not to hurt her—not seriously, anyway. In sex games, sure. But no woman has actually been afraid of me before. They've known I was dangerous, but that's part of the appeal right? Some women have particularly dangerous tastes in men. They like the wildness, that animal edge that so many men have lost. And I'd become accustomed to the jaded nature of these women who somehow trusted that I wouldn't turn my darkness against them—that somehow because they were hot and I was fucking them, that they were safe.

And to be fair, they were right. Women are in a different category for me from men. For all my violence, outside of sex games, none of that gets turned on women. And yet. Macy isn't like the others. She's actually afraid I will physically harm her. This is the part where I'm supposed to feel guilty, and where if I had an actual soul I would feel guilty. I feel *something*, but it's not guilt. It's more like the intoxicating feeling of power finding a new way to express itself.

And because of this, Macy may be as dangerous to me as I am to her.

I tell myself I didn't start her training last night because it was so late. She was tired. I was tired. And I have all the time in the world. But I'm not sure if that's the reason. I don't want to call it mercy because I don't think it was that. Maybe it was just a stay of execution. Or maybe I wanted to be well rested and fresh before starting.

I'm not sure if I'm going to hurt her, but the prognosis isn't good. Her tears make me hard. Her pleading whimpers fill me with a sense of power. But were she to stop crying and pleading, I might punish her for taking these small pleasures away from me. I'm fucked up. And she's just fucked.

Her entrance startles me mid-pacing. I turn and suck in a sharp breath as I take in the exquisite delicate loveliness that is Macy Laine. She's wearing the robe from from the bathroom and looks afraid I might rip it off her. And honestly, if she were one of the girls who'd come here to temporarily play the roll of toy, I might have done just that. I might have allowed her to blush and be horrified by Jeffrey walking in and staying a bit longer than necessary to do whatever task he was there to pretend to complete, all so he could take long lingering looks at my newest nude on display.

Jeffrey likes to watch and sometimes touch. And I like audiences, so... it works out. And it's always gotten my play-things worked up, making them that much more warm and wet for me to slide inside.

Beneath my greed for Macy, I know that if I push her too far too soon, I could break this new toy. I could end up with another hollow shell. And then there would be two of us without souls wandering the world lost. I need her to still be something so I can exist inside the energy I don't have the power to create within myself. She makes me feel... things.

I don't know what those things are. They're too foreign and rare to put a label on, but it's something more than I've ever felt. I don't know if it's because I now own someone, or if it's something about her specifically. I just know that when I touched her throat last night, I felt the way she relaxed under my hand. And it did something to me that I'm not sure can be undone.

Of all the reactions she could have had, this one unnerves me because it's not what she should feel. I'd expected her to pull away, to beg, maybe even to scream. I expected to see disgust, fear, and revulsion in her eyes. But she just breathed until her breath flowed into mine and mine flowed into hers. And for the first time ever in my life I felt a connection to another living creature.

I felt like there was something alive and pulsing inside me after all.

Half of me wants to hurt her for making me feel this thing. And there's the fear my weakness may give her power. The other half of me just wants to experience it again.

I realize suddenly that I've been standing here lost in my thoughts about this girl while she's looking at the floor and shivering even though she's in a long-sleeved robe and the house is plenty warm. Jeffrey turned on the in-floor heating an hour ago so even her bare feet won't get cold.

But on taking a second look at her I realize why she must be cold. Her hair is wet, probably from the shower.

I go to the bar and make myself a plate and return to the table. Macy still stands, tense and uncertain. I know she's waiting for me to comment on the robe, to make some demand that she remove it. But I don't.

"You should get some food before it gets cold."

I watch as she notices the food for the first time. She's not used to a spread like this. She's impressed, and I'd be lying if I said I wasn't a little pleased by this. So many of the women who come here are so jaded by wealth. Nothing impresses them. They're jaded by money. They're jaded by kink. They're jaded by the entire spectrum of male sexuality. They may not offer every single service on their menu, but they've heard it all. And every reaction to every thing feels calculated to please the client.

Macy tries to hide her reaction to the china. I'm sure that to Macy this is what many people call "the good china", but in my world, it's just the plates I eat off of every day. There is no "good china" that just comes out for company. All the china is the good china because there's no reason to use or have low quality anything, which reminds me, someone's going to have to take her shopping for suitable clothes if she's going to be Mrs. Black. Or we could have all her clothes custom tailored.

Macy watches me like a spooked doe as she eats. Jeffrey comes in and pours us some coffee, then he disappears again.

"I-I don't drink coffee," she says almost too quiet for me to hear, as though she's afraid I'll hurt her for not being a coffee drinker.

"Oh? What do you drink?"

"Tea."

Oh, Jeffrey will love her. He's been trying to get me to drink tea for years. "Jeffrey, Ms. Laine would like some tea."

On hearing this, he bounds into the kitchen like a puppy, as thrilled as I knew he'd be by this request.

"I have Earl Grey, English Breakfast, Irish Breakfast, Darjeeling..."

Before Jeffrey can rattle off the likely hundreds of teas he's been hoarding for god knows what reason, Macy says, "English breakfast, please."

Jeffrey takes away her coffee and goes to work on the tea. She continues to focus on her food, avoiding my gaze. Then she does the strangest thing. She picks up the saucer and turns it over to inspect the bottom of it.

Is she looking for a brand name? A price label? Could I have a gold digger hostage of all things?

"I knew it. Bone," she says as if satisfied by this knowledge.

"Excuse me?" I ask.

"Do you know the difference between fine china and bone china?"

I have no idea what to say to this so I just shake my head.

"Bone china has cow bone ash in it. It's what gives it the softer warmer color and translucence. But it's no stronger than fine china. That's a misnomer. It's just a way to alter the color."

"And how do you know this?" I still can't believe that the first non-terrified thing she's decided to say to me is about the difference in fine and bone china. I didn't know the difference—largely because I don't care—but I'm fascinated she just opened her mouth to tell me this. Maybe I seem less scary in the daylight.

"Livia didn't know when we were registering for her china for her wedding, and so I looked it up. I like bone better because it just looks more elegant to me. It's not as harsh."

Her face falls, and I know immediately what she's thinking. She's thinking she won't get to register for a china pattern for the wedding that won't be happening now. I don't know why, but this crestfallen look on her face bothers me.

Jeffrey brings her tea, then disappears again. She seems to suddenly realize she's been explaining the finer points of china content to her captor, and the discomfort and anxiety returns to her face as she distracts herself with her tea.

We finish eating in silence and Jeffrey takes the plates away. When the table has been cleared, she looks a bit awkward then starts to get up. I place my hand over hers, stopping her retreat.

"Sit. We have business to discuss."

"W-what kind of business?"

It hasn't escaped my notice that she hasn't called me what I told her to call me, but I decide to leave that for the moment. I take the stack of papers from the nearby island and place it on the table in front of her.

"This little arrangement protects Soren's stock prices from falling, and it also helps me. I need a Mrs. Black to make me look more normal and family-oriented. You will fulfill that role."

Her eyes go wide. "I-is this a pre-nup?"

"No. I have no interest in getting into a threeway with the state. This is a private contract that is meant to protect you and provide for you should I at any point choose to discard you. It was Soren's condition for giving you to me. It goes without saying that you won't be initiating an end to our arrangement. And, as stipulated in the contract, you will of course be giving me heirs."

She slides the papers across the table and crosses her arms over her chest. "I'm not signing this."

I'm surprised by this rebellion but I don't let it show on my face. "Not today you aren't. It'll be several weeks before I can take you out in public, and then we'll sign them properly at the attorney's office. I'm just informing you."

"No. You can keep me captive, but you can't make me sign these papers pretending a relationship we don't have."

I can't stop my eye roll. "Don't be ridiculous. These papers protect you. And from what I hear from Soren, you don't love the man you were going to be marrying anyway. So what difference does it make? My offer is better than his."

"You can't absolve your guilt by giving me the security of marriage. We're not in the Victorian age."

I place my palms flat on the table and lean forward so that I'm towering over her. "I don't feel guilt. You are mine, and this is a gift. And I really do need a Mrs. Black."

She shakes her head. "I'm not signing them."

"You'll sign them if I have to break you into a shell of your former self. You *will* sign them." I don't know what's come over me. I don't threaten women this way. I thought it was my one redeeming quality, but maybe it's just that no one's been brazen enough to challenge me.

"No."

"What happened to the girl who begged me not to hurt her last night?"

"She got some sleep and some food."

She's actually glaring at me as she says this.

"Great. So I only need to starve and sleep deprive you, and you'll be ready to sign? It's not the best idea to reveal all your weaknesses to me. Don't think I won't use them to get what I want."

A flicker of last night's fear moves over her face, and I'm satisfied this is only a bluff and boundary testing. It's her *attempt* to fight back, so she can say she tried and feel good about it. Fine. I'll let her have it.

"When were you supposed to be marrying this other uninspiring joker?"

"M-March twenty-eighth."

"March twenty-eighth," I repeat. "We'll be legally bound long before that, but I've got nothing planned that day if you want to have a wedding. Though you'll have to break it off with the other guy first. It might be awkward if we both showed up."

She stares at me like she can't tell if I'm serious or fucking with her. I can't believe it, but I'm actually serious. I'm taking everything from this girl—the life she knew, her choices, even her choice in who to marry. If she wants a wedding, well it's already partly planned, why not just trade out the groom?

While she's still caught off guard, I pull her phone from my pocket and place it on the table. "You said you wanted to call your friend."

She stares at it then back up at me. "Are you crazy? You know you're committing a felony right? And you're just letting me use a phone? Why not go ahead and mail your fingerprints to the FBI?"

I shrug. "You said she'd worry, and you're going to have to be able to be taken out in public eventually. It's an opportunity for you to start building trust with me. I suggest you take it. Do you need me to show you the dungeon to give you incentive not to screw me over?"

She shakes her head quickly.

"Good. Put it on speaker."

# 7

## MACY

I stare at my phone as Colin slides it across the table like it's some kind of trick, like if I reach out for it I'll get an electric zap. Finally I do reach for it. Just as my hand closes over it, his hand closes over mine. I gasp like a school girl at the contact.

Why is his touch so warm and soothing? I shouldn't feel so safe when he touches me. If we were animals out in the wild, this would be a predator thing like *look it's pretty, oh it's poison!* And even though I'm smart enough to know this in the way you know things out of a book, a deeper part of me doesn't know it and can't be convinced.

*How can something this attractive be bad*, the stupid part of my brain says.

I keep having to remind myself we aren't on a date. I shouldn't have to remind myself this, but in your average kidnapping situation you don't get brunch on the fancy plates with a butler making you tea. Plus Colin, while just as intense as before is starting to feel Soren-storm intense— which is comforting because it's familiar. Also, he's neither in shadows nor looming over me and glaring right now so

I'm feeling maybe one percent less scared and ten percent more turned on.

And I hate myself with every fiber of my being for thinking this thought but he is so much hotter than Will, which seems like one of those evil tricks the universe plays. Colin is obviously... financially comfortable would be the polite way to say it. And if he doesn't murder me, he might be into the things I *think* I'm into. How does one know what they're truly into if they haven't done anything yet?

I've also fantasized about sky-diving or being an international spy, and I can say for sure I don't want to do those things in real life. I think. Plus this isn't a game, something I keep having to remind myself of because he's so hot it's hard to remember someone so beautiful is actually a monster.

"Where are your manners?" he asks, interrupting what otherwise would be a never ending rambling monologue in my head. Trust me, I can make it go for days.

My bravado of *you can't make me do anything because I ate food and slept and now feel like a super hero* from only a few minutes ago has completely shattered under both his steady touch and gaze.

"I-I'm sorry?" I say.

"What do you say when someone does something nice for you?"

"Thank you?" I say it like it's a question on a test I didn't study for.

He raises an eyebrow at me, and I know what he's searching for. I know what he wants me to say, but if I say it I'm afraid of how my body will react. I'm barely holding myself together right now. And I'm not sure what falling apart would entail in this moment.

It could mean crying hysterically, or unrestrained lust. Either reaction creates danger for me. If I cry nonstop he might decide I'm too much trouble and throw me into a volcano for real. But if I allow myself to be drawn to the pretty poison, that's not much better.

He's still waiting, and I decide maybe I should try to buy a bit of grace instead of acting like a little idiot who can't remember a simple conversation.

"Thank you, Master," I finally say. It takes every bit of internal strength I have not to look down when I say this. I need to see his reaction to distract me from my own.

His eyes darken with lust as that all-important word falls from my mouth.

"Good girl." His voice is a low gravel rumble more effective than a vibrator.

He finally removes his hand from mine, and I can breathe again. I take the phone and call Livia, trying to control the tremble in my fingers as I scroll to her name on my contact list. As directed, I put the call on speaker.

"Oh my god, Macy. I've tried calling you sixteen thousand times today. It's after noon. Did you go for marathon masturbation this morning or just sleep in because you don't work on Monday?"

"Livia!" is all I can say. But I know my face is burning hot. I can't help glancing up again just in time to see Colin's eyebrow go up along with the smirk that slides across his face.

"Wait... am I on speaker?"

"Yes, you're on speaker."

"Oops, sorry. Who else is there?"

"No one," I say quickly. "I'm just getting ready, and it's easier."

"Okay, then answer the question... and if it was a marathon, which of your dirty kinky fantasies got you there? Because all three of the guys are going on some trip to do some merger that somehow involves all of them, but I don't get to go, so I need to understand your methods to get me through this twenty-four hour drought."

Colin is actively having to fight laughter. The only good thing about this is it drops my fear by another ten percentage points. If he'd mentioned me being Mrs. Black right now instead of before, I might have been tempted. Or at least I wouldn't have outright refused. I mean, I *did* say yes to Will, and that was just as stupid. Apparently I'll marry anybody who can put those words together in a sentence.

"Why did you call so many times?" I ask, trying to get Livia off the topic of my masturbation habits.

"I wanted to know which dress you ended up getting for the wedding."

Livia had to leave before I decided and bought the dress because she had to meet Griffin and Dayne for dinner. The mystery of why Soren wasn't going to be there was solved by me, though I obviously can't tell her what her legal-on-paper husband was doing while Griffin and Dayne were distracting her. It makes me wonder if the other two guys are mixed up in this situation too.

"I got the dark green one," I say.

"Good choice. I think that'll look great with your hair and eyes. I always thought you'd go with the traditional white, though."

My awareness of Colin's scrutiny is the only thing that keeps me from launching into the Queen Victoria story about white wedding dresses. I really want to explain how short a time period white dresses have been traditional. This need to knowledge dump is like an itch I can't scratch. But I already nerded out earlier when I for some reason felt it necessary to tell the man keeping me as his slave the difference in fine and bone china. I cannot let him see this is a real personality feature of mine and not just some nervous tick.

"So was that all you wanted?" I ask not sure what the hell else to say to her with an audience and too afraid of what else she may say to let her keep talking on speaker.

"Yeah, and hey, do you want to sleep over tonight? I'll be all alone in this big house."

I look up, already knowing what I'll find when I do. Colin is shaking his head, reminding me why I should hate him instead of feel attraction for him. He thinks he owns me. And technically, if I can't find a way to escape, I guess he does. But in the light of day I'm starting to feel more optimistic about figuring out an escape route.

"I can't," I say.

"Of course you can. You don't have to work tomorrow. Just come over. We'll order pizza. Also... if you're wearing green, what color am I wearing?"

I feel too flustered under Colin's gaze to discuss wedding plans for a wedding that isn't happening, and I don't know how to get out of this conversation.

"Someone's at the door, I have to call you back." I end the call before she can say anything else.

"No," Colin says, his arms crossed over his chest.

"No, what?" I assume he's going to explain to me why I can't see my friend, which really is pretty obvious to me since he's breaking the law to keep me locked away in his castle.

"No, you're not wearing a green dress. You're wearing white like a proper bride."

"There isn't going to be a wedding," I say. And somewhere in the back of my mind I always knew this was true. I think I just wanted to pretend for a little while longer and plan even though I knew I couldn't go through with it. It's probably the real reason I got a dark green dress.

I'm not a total rule follower but I'm not a big breaker of tradition either. The dress was non-refundable, but it just looks like a formal gown. Nothing about it screams wedding, so I knew I could always save it and wear it to some other function later—not that I typically attend fancy functions like that but you never know. These white lies allowed me do some wedding shopping while still planning my exit strategy.

But now, given my current situation, there really isn't going to be a wedding.

"Yes there is," Colin says. "I told you we'll have one."

At first I think he just read my mind but then remember I actually DID say that that out loud before I started over-thinking again.

"How would that even work? I can't just trade out the groom!" I say, finally.

"Why not? You haven't sent out invitations have you? If I recall correctly from my sister's wedding, invitations don't go out until much closer to the date. Did you send out save the date cards?"

"No... but..."

He has a sister? How in the hell does that work? How does a man like this have a sister and still do what he's doing?

"Do you have anything on order with both of your names printed on it?" he prods.

"No... but..."

"But nothing. You're getting married on March twenty-eighth."

"To my captor," I say, probably with more sarcasm than is wise.

"Yes." There is no sense of irony or humor in his tone. He is dead serious. "I told you, I need a Mrs. Black. A wedding makes it look less like the business equivalent of a green card marriage."

"I have to keep my last name," I say as though I'm just

going along with this. But what good will fighting him do? I need to be agreeable, earn his trust, and then escape when he lets me go out. He said he's going to let me leave the house at some point. So when he does, that's when I can escape.

"Since it's not a marriage license marriage, that's fine," he says, relieving me of having to explain my mental rabbit trail of why I can't be Macy Black. It would sound like I'm trying to be a pop star.

"You're going to have to come up with a reason to tell Livia that you won't be able to see her for a few weeks."

I open my mouth to speak but then close it again. Finally I say, "There's nothing I can say that she'll believe. I see her too frequently and she knows me too well."

"What about a business trip?" he suggests.

"I'm a research librarian. My business trips are to the locked reference floor where we keep the expensive old books."

"A vacation then."

I shake my head. "I don't really travel. And Livia would want to come too."

"Sick relative."

"Nope. I'm not on speaking terms with my family."

He doesn't ask why, and I'm glad. I don't like to talk about it. The short version is they're kind of scummy scam artists and I got tired of bailing them all out with money I don't have so I moved to the other side of the country and changed my number. The entire family has this get-rich-quick mentality, and they're all obsessed with money in the way that people who play the lottery every time they go to the gas station are obsessed with money.

I couldn't live like that anymore. I'm the only member of my family who is responsible with money. I don't even know how or where I got this personality trait. Maybe I was switched at birth. An evil part of me kind of wants to reconnect with them now that Colin is demanding I be Mrs. Black. I wonder how fast he'd let me go if my entire family started coming after him for money and investment advice.

"What are you smiling about?" he looks suspicious.

"Nothing."

"Friends?" he asks.

"Huh?"

"Do you have any friends you could say you were visiting or helping in some way?"

"I'm kind of an introvert. Most of the time I don't spend with Livia, I spend at work at the library."

Colin sighs. "So you're telling me the only people in the world who will miss you are your work and Livia?"

I nod slowly, not at all liking where this conversation is going.

"I know a lot of people," I interject. "University staff, all the library people, lots of regulars who come in, Professors, Visiting professors..."

I trail off at Colin's raised eyebrow. It's probably for the best because I was close to mentioning the people who work in the campus bookstore and the janitorial staff.

I look down at my empty plate and take one more sip of the tea before it gets too cool to drink. Finally, Colin stands. I feel the heavy weight of his gaze on me.

"Come with me, Miss Laine."

I look up to find his hand outstretched, something which would be a gallant gesture in any other situation with any other person. I take a moment to really take in the suit porn in front of me, and I feel extremely underdressed.

"Where are we going?" I ask, and immediately wish I hadn't.

"I need to punish you."

# 8

## COLIN

I don't know why I said I *needed* to punish her. Shouldn't I have said *want* instead? Or I could have simply stated I was *going* to punish her. But as I assess the situation I realize that yes, need was accurate. I need to punish her, and she needs to be punished.

My shoulder is still sore this morning from the vase she threw at me. She ran from me and damn near got herself killed. She was belligerent. She danced around the title I demanded, and she said she wasn't going to marry me. Like hell she isn't. I think that last thing is what pisses me off the most.

Scores of women have tried in vain to get to be Mrs. Black, and Macy—the one woman I wouldn't mind having in my space long term—turned me down. Not that her refusal means anything. She'll still sign the papers one way or another. We will be contractually bound, and she will be mine.

She already is mine.

And Soren will get to keep all his dirty little secrets tucked away for another day.

Macy's hand trembles as she places it in mine. Her breath hitches in her throat. I don't say anything else to her —no words of reassurance. Better to start her initiation into my world now before she gets too comfortable. Besides, didn't her friend mention kinky fantasies? What darkness lurks in the mind of my sweet little virgin?

I lead her out of the bright kitchen and down a few hallways, each darker than the last as we move further and further from the natural light of windows and into the artificial light of dim wall sconces. I input a code at a door at the end of the hall, and it slides open. I guide Macy down the stairs into my fully equipped sex dungeon.

I let go of her hand when we get down to the lower level. I expect her to bolt, but she just stands there, taking in the array of bondage furniture, whipping implements, and toys.

"Take off the robe."

But she only pulls it closed over her.

"Are we going to do this again, Macy? I've seen you naked." And she seemed very confused by why I haven't fucked her yet. She is mine, after all. A sacrifice all wrapped up for me to devour at my leisure.

She blushes in the way that only a redhead can do.

"Close your eyes," I say when she makes no move to obey my previous order. She's shy, and unbelievably I think this is less about what I might do to her down here and more uncertainty... about herself? Her desirability? I mean I *am* the monster here.

Obviously I want her. I'm doing crime to keep her. And it's too warm down here for her nipples poking through that robe to be anything but arousal. So I know her hesitance isn't repulsion at the idea of me looking at her.

After another moment's hesitation, she closes her eyes. I pull a blindfold from my pocket and secure it in place. I can be merciful. I can make this easier for her. I find my hand stroking the column of her throat. A tiny sigh escapes her mouth as she leans close to me.

I stare at that mouth. I want her on her knees and that mouth wrapped greedily around my cock. I shake that thought from my head. Not yet. I want to do this right. I'm keeping this one.

My hand trails across her collarbone and down until it closes over her hand, still clasping the robe. Her grip releases under my touch, and she lets me pull first one hand, then the other down by her sides. The robe falls open and I push it over her shoulders and let it fall to the floor.

My gaze moves downward, and I'm shocked to find her bare. Perhaps I should have noticed this before, but it wasn't clear in the bath. And when she came out, I kept the room mostly dark to ease her into my world.

"When did you get waxed?"

"T-the other day," she says after only a moment's pause.

"I thought you were a virgin."

She blushes harder at this.

"I am."

"Were you planning to do something to solve that little problem? Who were you planning on showing your pretty pussy to?"

"No. N-no one. That's not why I wax."

I swear my eyebrow is going to get stuck in its current position of surprise. "If you don't wax for a man, why do you wax?"

I'm sure if she wasn't able to hide behind the blindfold she wouldn't answer me.

But she takes a deep breath and says, "For me."

I think about that for a moment. Does she like the way it looks? The way it feels? Does she prefer to touch herself without any hair in the way? Or is she a masochist? Does she like the pain? Or the endorphin rush afterward? I once knew a girl who kept regular waxing appointments to keep panic attacks at bay. She said the endorphin rush after made her calmer than even a massage could do.

I don't ask Macy to elaborate. I let the mystery be as I take in her small perfectly proportioned breasts, pink nipples, the feminine flare of her hips. The gentle softness of her belly.

It takes me a moment to realize I'm holding my breath. I've lost track of the number of naked women I've seen. It shouldn't still have the power to stun me, but there's something different in Macy's beauty, something uncomplicated, untouched, and uninitiated. Something sweet and innocent and new.

I notice she removed the bandages. Her minor injuries from last night don't look nearly as bad in the day. The cuts have closed and they aren't as angry and red as I expected them to be this morning. Even with these marks though, there's space for me to leave my own.

I have a moment of weakness where I'm not sure if I can bring myself to leave marks on her. But this feeling passes as quickly as it came, leaving behind the hunger that demands to be sated.

"Macy?"

"Y-yes, Master?"

But I don't answer her. I just wanted to know if she would persist in resisting the title I demand. I take her hand and guide her to the center of the room. She doesn't say anything or fight me when I raise her arms over her head and bind them together with soft leather cuffs hanging from the ceiling. She's standing on her toes.

"What size shoes do you wear?" I can't have her standing like that for long.

"Ummm, six?"

"Is that a question?"

"No, Master. Six."

I keep black heels in multiple sizes for these situations and 3 inches should be perfect to keep her off her toes.

"M-Master?" she says, sounding panicked when she hears me walk away.

"I'm not leaving you," I reassure her. I retrieve a pair of heels in her size from a large leather trunk and help her into them.

I spread her legs and cuff her into a spreader bar so she can't close them, then I stand back to take in her beauty and subtle curves. How is it possible that I'm the first man here?

"Have you ever been punished? As an adult?" I want to make it clear I'm not asking about childhood spankings. Just because she's a virgin doesn't mean she can't have done other things, though that seems unlikely if Soren was the first man who's seen her naked. I find myself irrationally jealous of this, even though I made that call.

"No, Master," she says barely above a whisper.

I move into her space, pressing myself against her naked body. I snake an arm around her allowing my fingertips to dance up and down her spine. I brush away her still-damp fiery hair and leave a soft kiss where her neck meets her shoulder. She shudders at this.

I hold her around her lower back so her arms don't have to support her full weight. I'm sure she feels my erection pressing against her belly through my suit.

"I'll give you nine if you cry pretty for me and ten if you try too hard to be brave."

Her lip is already quivering.

I should start her with the riding crop or a flogger, but I want to leave cane welts. I want to leave a strong first impression.

I stroke her soft ass, and a whispering moan escapes her. I'm surprised she hasn't begged or struggled or fought.

There is a part of Macy that wants to find out what happens, and I'm more than happy to allow her this discovery.

I let go of her and go to the box to retrieve the cane.

"You will count them," I say when I return.

She shrieks on the first one. Definitely a kink virgin.

"O-One."

I use more restraint on two through five. She silently cries through all of them as she counts. She hasn't begged yet. I'm not sure if I'm pleased or disappointed by this... if I should reward her or punish her harder.

Six is harder.

"M-Master, Please!"

There it is. The air is electric between us. "What number, Macy?"

"S-six, Master."

"Good girl."

"Please, please, please..."

I have never in my life shown more mercy than I said up front I would offer, but her tears are doing things to me. Both good things and bad things, and I can't separate and detangle these feelings. I can't decide if I want to keep going or if I want to stop. But I don't do mercy. I don't do kindness. I don't do restraint.

"Three more," I growl.

She's sobbing now. Maybe it's relief that I'm stopping at nine instead of the ten I threatened if she didn't "cry pretty" for me.

I pull back a little for seven and eight, but nine is as hard as the first, bringing that shriek out of her again. She has counted each one. Such a good girl.

I put the cane down and stand back to admire the welts I left on her. I stroke her back and move closer to leave a hungry, biting kiss at her throat.

My lips brush against her ear as I whisper, "I'm going to make you feel so many things, Macy."

Her reply is a whimper.

I remove the blindfold and when I look into her pale green eyes, I know without any doubt this girl is mine. Not because Soren brought her to me. Not because of any sordid plan. No, she's mine in a far deeper way. There is a thrumming, a hum hidden below the frequency of civilization... a primal place that exists in the recesses of long-forgotten memory. That is where Macy and I live together and why she is mine.

My gaze drifts from hers, down to her lips. I consider claiming her mouth but I don't. I don't want to break the intimacy or the energy of what we just shared together with a romantic cherry on a sundae. It would soften things. It would break things.

Instead, I reach up and unbind her wrists, rubbing them. "Pins and needles?" I ask.

"No, Master." Her voice is so quiet.

She rests her hands on my shoulders as I bend to uncuff her ankles from the spreader bar. I don't even think she realizes she's doing it.

Then I stand, pick her up, and carry her up the stairs. Maybe she can walk, but I want to carry her. She's so slight that it isn't a burden to take her up a couple flights of stairs to my bedroom. She burrows her head in my neck.

I carry her past staff, past Jeffrey whose eyes greedily drink their fill of her as we pass.

I lay her across my king-sized bed.

"Roll onto your stomach."

She obeys, and I go get something to put on her welts. When I return she's crying again. I don't ask why. I don't want to break this with words. I've whipped a lot of women. I've caned a lot of women. I've fucked a lot of women, and I've never experienced anything like what just happened in the dungeon. There are no words to convey it.

It was such a small slice of time, and yet a lifetime of experience was poured into it.

I'm not good with words. Or feelings. Or really anything civil or human. I can pretend. I can put on the mask as any other man might put on his suit and tie and go to the office. Do normal men still even wear suits and ties to the office? Or is it all Zoom calls and Every Day Casual Friday, now?

I'm sure Macy felt it, too. But I don't ask her. I let myself believe that we shared something deeper than I've ever shared with a sub in my dungeon before today. I want to tell myself it's just that it's new. I've merely fed off her energy like a vampire takes blood. But I'm not sure that's it. I don't think it's her lack of experience.

I think it's her.

I stroke the marks. They criss-cross over her ass and thighs. I run my tongue over the grooves and welts. When I rub aloe gel into them, she can't hold back the moan.

Finally I can't take it anymore. I have to know. I move my hand between her legs to find her dripping for me.

I roll her onto her back and press my mouth to her bare pussy. She jumps, surprised. Her breathing deepens as she watches me. I take my time tasting her, spreading her open with my fingers, fingering her while I suck and lick and kiss her small bud.

I raise my gaze to hers. "Are you going to come for me like a good girl?"

She swallows hard, but only nods. I don't chastise her for the lack of title. I don't think her words work right now.

I return her nod and go back to work between her legs. She tastes as sweet as I knew she would. She lets out these soft desperate pants as I drive her closer and closer to the edge. My hands dig into her thighs, pulling her greedily toward me. I'm sure I'll leave hand marks, but I don't care.

Her hips buck against my mouth, and she comes apart as I devour her.

When it's over, I stand and straighten my tie. I hold her gaze as I wipe her remaining wetness away. A soft knock interrupts the moment, and Jeffrey steps inside. If I weren't holding Macy's gaze, I think she'd try to cover up, but she doesn't dare. I feel Jeffrey staring at her, but still, she doesn't dare.

"Soren is on the phone for you, Sir."

"Thank you."

Jeffrey excuses himself, and I follow him out into the hall, closing the door behind me.

# 9

## MACY

I lay in Colin's bed, panting, trying to will my heartbeat back down to a normal cadence instead of the galloping horses seeking to break free of my chest. I feel ashamed at how easily I surrendered my pleasure to him. It took so very little for him to draw out my orgasm, to have me open and willing, spread out before him like a gift. Like a sacrifice. Just as he said.

No man has ever touched me like this. Aside from some kissing and awkward teenage fumbling, no man has ever touched me at all. Despite my fantasies, my very brief encounters left me wondering if sex was even that big of a deal at all. Even with Livia's gushing details, I wasn't entirely convinced. Now I am.

I'd walked into the room afraid he'd rape me, and within twenty minutes I was desperate for him to be inside me. But it didn't get that far. Colin was pulled away by a phone call. He took the call in the hallway and although I couldn't make out many words, his serious tone was clear.

I pull the sheet up over myself, suddenly very conscious of my nudity. What am I doing? What's *wrong* with me? I'm lying here like a little idiot fantasizing about my captor. This man is dangerous. This psycho thinks I'm his property. I'm angry at myself for giving in so easily. It took so very little for me to spread my legs for him. Even after the punishment, I shouldn't have been this willing to give myself to him.

I reason with myself that it's an extreme situation. I've been through a lot in the past twenty-four hours. Of course I'd want to appease someone this powerful and dangerous. Of course I would rather have pleasure than pain.

Before all of this I used to read romance novels with heroines captured by the hero. They would always fight so hard and end up getting hurt or punished in some awful way. The stories were easier to brush off when it was fantastical creatures like vampires and werewolves, but it seemed even stupider to me then that the heroine would ever behave in this way as though she had some latent super power that would emerge at just the right moment to save the day.

Even so, when I talked about these books with other readers online, they would always be so annoyed the heroine didn't fight back harder, not shy to tell us all what they would do in her place. I never said what I really felt about all that.

I threw a vase at Colin and ran. I took the opportunity I had. But now I know how futile fighting and running is. Now I can see how complete my cage is, how large his power. There's nowhere to run. I've already seen that first hand when I almost froze to death in the woods last night. I'm lucky something didn't come along and eat me. I still have the scrapes to prove the stupidity of my brief bravery.

If I were a heroine in a novel, all my online friends would be mad at me and calling me weak saying I didn't try hard enough, and there has to be a way out. I think they'd feel differently if they were really here in this position. Life isn't a novel or a movie. Their bravery would evaporate much more quickly than mine did. Most people just want to be safe, and hardly anyone is brave when it really counts.

It's so stupid for me to care what an online book club called Shameless Stockholm Syndrome Addicts would think of me. But maybe they're right. Maybe there is a way out. Maybe I *haven't* tried hard enough. Couldn't I find car keys and escape? There's a gate on the property. I don't know the code to get out. But... I could find the code, find some keys, get in the car and...

My nonsensical escape fantasies are interrupted by the sound of Colin speaking more loudly now.

"Pack my bags. I need to be in the air in two hours."

"And the girl?" Jeffrey asks.

I stop breathing in the long pause, waiting to hear my fate.

"I'll handle the girl."

"Yes, Sir," Jeffrey says.

Then there's silence for several long minutes. Finally, Colin enters the room and drops some clothes on the bed—my clothes.

"Did I tell you you could cover yourself?" he asks.

"N-no, Master."

I don't forget the title. I won't forget the title ever again. I can't even convince myself that I find it horrible to say these words when I've touched myself night after night to this very scenario. No matter how afraid I am, no matter how much I know I'm not truly safe, my body can't be convinced that this isn't everything I've ever wanted. Every nerve ending hums with the thrill of the final consummation of all my needs and desires. Well, maybe not all of them, not yet. But I know it's coming, and I know I'll open my legs to him just as easily when he's there to take instead of give.

He arches a brow at me, and I slowly pull back the sheet

to let him see what he wants to see. I feel my entire body flush as his heated gaze scans each inch of my flesh, finally stopping to take in the exposed juncture between my thighs. I'm so wet I know he can easily still see it in the full bright light of day.

"It's a shame I don't have more time with you," he says finally on a sigh.

My heartbeat picks up speed. A low internal alarm starting to sound. What does that mean?

"A-are you letting me go?"

He shakes his head. "Macy, I told you I'm never letting you go."

It feels as though a heavy stone has settled in my stomach. It pins me in place, and I can't move. The tears stream down my cheeks as if on cue.

"M-master, please. Please, I don't want to die. Please, I... I won't say anything. I won't... "

I flinch as he moves forward, his finger presses against my lips. "Shhhh. I have business to take care of. I can't take you with me, and I'm not leaving you alone with Jeffrey. He only has so much self control. Don't let his formal British accent fool you."

Colin opens a drawer in the night stand and takes out a gleaming silver bracelet. It's solid and sturdy. Heavy looking. He locks it around my wrist with a small key.

"Listen to me very carefully. You're going back to your life for a little while. You will not utter a single word about me. The bracelet is waterproof. There's a microphone, a transmitter, and a tracker embedded inside. If you try to take it off, disable it in any way, or try to escape me, well... I'd be sorry to lose you. I will collect you when I'm ready for you. Get dressed and Jeffrey will drive you home."

Colin stands and drops my cell phone on the bed beside me. He watches me for several agonizing seconds as I allow what he's just said to sink in. The horror of the implied threat is eclipsed by the silver lining. I get to go home. I can see Livia! I've still got a job. I've only been gone for the weekend, after all. No one will even know I was missing.

Like this is the part to focus on. Whoo, I get to go back to work at the library! What a sad, sheltered life. Even after kidnapping and the best orgasm I've ever had, I'm still craving the dusty reference books. I even want to slap myself.

"Are you going to be a good girl for me while I'm gone, Macy?"

"Y-yes, Master."

But my mind is spinning. Is there really a microphone? I can see a small pinhole in the bracelet. Maybe? Or maybe it's all a lie. Maybe there's no microphone. No transmitter. No tracker. Maybe he's toying with me and just wants to see what I'll do. Maybe it amuses him to think he's put some completely powerless bracelet on me, and yet I'll be obeying and fearing and never touching it or trying to take it off for fear some spy of his will take me out with a sniper rifle.

Does he even have spies? I know he's bought at least part of the police force. Jeffrey doesn't care what he does. And Soren *gave* me to him. How many men does he have loyal to him?

Is he really going to just show up in a few days and take me back? It seems unlikely. Maybe he's lost interest—maybe something about me turned out to be not what he wanted after all. Maybe he's done with me and wants to see how long I'll keep his secret.

I'm not stupid. I don't run around spilling my guts about criminals. People who tell the secrets of criminals, die. And I'm sure this man has blood on his hands. What's one more body to him? There's something in his energy that feels like he and death are closely acquainted, good friends in fact.

Even so I can't help thinking about escape. Real escape. As much as my body has already begun to sing for him, I know he's not my fantasy. He's my doom. How can I not attempt escape? How can he trust or believe I won't do something stupid after I already ran from him last night?

"W-what am I supposed to do?" I ask.

"Go back to your life and live it normally. Spend time with with your friend. Go to your job. Plan your wedding."

I'd momentarily forgotten about Will and the wedding.

"I need to cancel the wedding," I say.

"No. You need to keep your life the same and not do anything different or strange. I will collect you when I'm ready for you."

"B-but I was going to cancel the wedding anyway. I can't marry Will. I don't love him."

Colin shakes his head. "Keep your life the same or I will punish you when I come to collect you."

This asshole. Come to collect me. My gaze darts around the room for another vase to chuck at him.

"If I say something you might kill me but the information will still be out there." Why would he take such a huge risk? But maybe it's not such a risk. Colin Black may not even be his real name. Maybe he has contingency plans. I don't know where we are or how to get here. What could I possibly say that would endanger him anyway?

He stops and pins me with a hard stare that makes me squirm, then he turns on his heel and leaves the room. I'm left gaping after him like a fish. My body is confused. I'm terrified but attracted. My brain is trying to interrupt this insanity to remind me that I've been kidnapped and this isn't a rom com. But the space between my legs reacts like Pavlov's dog to his intensity and the way he touched me.

His touch brings me comfort and pleasure even as everything else about him warns of my impending death.

And while I'm scared he'll make good on his promise and come collect me when he's finished doing whatever he's got to go do that's so important, I'm almost equally afraid that he won't come collect me and I'll be standing at the altar with William, sealing my fate to a man who I know won't be able to make me feel a tenth of what this man just did. And he got interrupted. He wasn't even *done* with me yet.

I try to remind myself that isn't the part to focus on.

I can't marry Will. Not after what just happened with Colin—not after getting a taste of the passion that's possible. I mean... I don't want Colin. Colin is crazy and evil. I want someone who can make me feel the way Colin just made me feel but in a safe environment. I repeat these thoughts over and over in my mind until they almost start to sound true, until I can almost believe I mean them.

I struggle to pull myself out of bed and put on the clothes he left for me. A few minutes later there's a soft knock on the door.

"Miss Laine?" Jeffrey calls in his proper British accent. "May I come in?"

I find it hard to believe Colin is worried about this guy touching me because his formal British butler routine doesn't exactly scream, *are you ready for me to take you to my secret sex dungeon?*

"Yes, come in."

The door opens. He looks me over and then hands me a black scrap of fabric.

"When we get in the car I'll need you to put the blindfold on. For security. You understand."

I follow him outside, my gaze scanning the house for my captor to no avail. *Do not look for him, Macy.* I chide myself. *Good riddance to the psycho. God only knows what he was going to do with you.* But something inside my chest already clenches at Colin's absence.

Jeffrey opens the back door of a vintage Rolls Royce for me and I slip inside, my hands pressing against the buttery leather seats.

"The blindfold, Ma'am," he says, reminding me of the scrap of fabric still tightly clenched in my hand.

I tie the blindfold around my eyes, then he gets into the driver's side and starts the car. I'm not even tempted to remove the blindfold. I assume Jeffrey is going to be watching me like a hawk through the rearview mirror. It's not worth it.

# 10

## MACY

It's Saturday, the first week of October. It's been almost two weeks since Colin let me go. If it weren't for the reminder of the weight of the bracelet, I'd have long convinced myself it was all a dream or some psychotic break with reality. Though for the first week, I had the reminder of the cane marks. I ran my fingertips over them and looked at them in the mirror, willing them to stay with me, even as they faded a bit each day.

Then I berated myself for thinking something so unhinged. And now even his marks are gone.

I've returned to work in the library—it's busy with the fall semester in full swing. And I've gone back to planning the wedding I don't want to have with the help of Livia who is none the wiser that I was ever gone.

As a good best friend does, she noticed there was something off about me, and she commented about the bracelet but I just made up a story about it being a gift from a friend. Though simple, it is quite pretty. It looks like an actual piece of jewelry rather than what it really is.

Once I'd gotten out into the sunlight with it, I could see

it was a gleaming silver metal with intricate etchings. It definitely doesn't make me look like a prisoner on house arrest. What if it *is* just a bracelet? I mean, yes, there's the tiny hole that could be the microphone, but what if it isn't? Or what if it's worse? What if it's a camera?

I know he said it's waterproof, but what does that mean, really? How are my daily showers not destroying it? Maybe it really is just a bracelet, and I'm living out my life waiting to be collected by a psychopath and afraid to speak or run because of an imaginary tether.

Is this his real game? Maybe there's no one watching me, no power in this bracelet at all but I'll end up wearing it for the rest of my days on the off chance that the moment I try to remove it a bullet will come sailing my way to end me. What a sociopath.

Despite all this, my daily masturbation schedule hasn't been thrown off even a little bit. If anything I'm doing it more. That one taste of pleasure with another living human ignited a fire in me. It's like getting a taste of a powerful drug and being unable to resist coming back for more. And more. And more. I'm afraid I'm hooked now.

If there's a microphone, who's listening? Is anyone listening? Do the blankets in my bed muffle the sounds of my moans? Does Colin listen? Does he hear me get off? Does he know that when I fantasize now, he's the one my mind can't forget?

With every passing day I wonder where he is and if he's coming back. I always expect my door to burst open, or to be taken off the street, even in broad daylight—such is the power I've convinced myself this man has.

I've taken to romanticizing my capture to a degree that frightens me. After all, what did he really do to me that was so terrible? He didn't personally kidnap me. Soren did that. He didn't throw me in a cell. He didn't beat or torture me. He didn't starve me. He didn't rape me. No everything he did on that score was fully desired—much to my shame.

When I tried to escape, he didn't hurt me. He got me warm, fed me, cleaned me up, and dressed my wounds. He gave me a warm bed instead of a cell or closet to sleep in. He fed me a nice brunch the next day in a sunlit kitchen where Jeffrey made me tea.

He *has* obliquely threatened to kill me or have me killed. So there's that. Obviously that douses the fantasy with a big bucket of frigid water. But I think that's just if I talk or try to get the bracelet off. *STOP rationalizing this.* Why haven't I gone to the police? Okay so maybe the police aren't safe but I could get help outside their jurisdiction. Surely they could trace the transmitter in the bracelet. They could find him.

But that's the problem. There is a terrible small sick part of me horrified by the idea of the police finding this man and taking him away. I should be committed to an institution, assuming there is such a place that would even know what to do with me.

But I can't forget the way his touch calmed me. I can't stop thinking about how it felt completely right to be touched by this man no matter how much he terrifies me or how wrong it is or how wrong he is. It doesn't matter how dangerous the flame is when its warmth keeps me from freezing.

It's too late to try to save myself because a part of me wants him to come back for me to save me from the horrible emptiness of a loveless and passionless marriage, my sentence which still looms over me. I want to cancel the wedding. I have far more fortitude to cancel it than I did before Colin took me, but he said no.

And I'm afraid to defy that order. I'm afraid to defy any order. I know that's not healthy. I know he's not my fairy tale prince. I spend every day just waiting for the monster to come out of the volcano and take his sacrifice. And that wait is just a little too eager. I want to talk to Livia about all this so badly. Maybe she'd understand. After all, didn't her relationship with her guys start out kind of the same? Or she could help me break the hold Colin seems to have over my mind and my libido.

But I can't say anything. What if his threats are real? And then I'd be dragging Livia into this, and she might be in danger too.

When I'm not worrying and obsessing about all this, I'm worried he hasn't come back because he can't come back. I'm worried something bad happened to him. What business did he have? Was it dangerous? Was it criminal? Was he killed or maybe arrested? Every day my anxiety climbs higher, equal parts fear he'll take me away from my boring safe life and fear that I'll never see him again. *I don't want to see him again.* But no matter how many times I force that thought through my mind, it never takes, it never feels real or true.

His cruel beauty haunts my dreams, and the memory of his touch sears my soul.

I was only with him for twenty-four hours. He can't have such a hold on me. Was I truly *that* lonely? And truly *that* stupid? Yes. I was that lonely—the perfect prey for a man like Colin Black. I try not to beat myself up about the stupid part. Loneliness can make you think and want stupid things.

The phone rings, jarring me out of my racing thoughts.

"Macy, where the fuck are you? We had an appointment to taste cake at three o'clock. It's five minutes after and Claudia is glaring daggers into me. If you're not here in fifteen minutes we'll lose the appointment. You know I had to pull strings to get it in the first place."

It's Livia. Shit.

"I'll be there in ten," I say. I hang up the phone, put my

hair up in a loose top knot and throw on a sweater and some jeans. The sweater goes off the shoulder, revealing a red bra strap which makes it look like I'm trying hard to look like I'm not trying hard to be sexy. But I don't have time to care about that.

The baker is only three blocks away, so I throw on some tennis shoes and jog the whole way. I'm out of breath when the bell rings over the door as I push it open.

"Sorry," I say, panting. I might really need to do some cardio if I can't even run three blocks.

Despite not wanting the wedding I'm still very lucky to get this appointment. Claudia is in huge demand for wedding cakes. The little cakes are already sitting out on the table waiting for me to taste and select. I don't know why we're even doing this. I should have just chosen what Livia chose. Lemon cake for the wedding, chocolate for the groom's cake. But I don't want to copy her. She's already tried to talk me into canceling this wedding about thirty more times.

"Get the strawberry," Livia says. "Remember how much we loved it but Soren's stupid uncle was allergic? Now I can have my dream strawberry cake!"

She raises and lowers her eyebrows at me in quick succession, and I can't help laughing. In an ordinary situation this might make her the worst matron of honor in the world, trying to vicariously live through my cake, but we both know this wedding with Will is a sham. It may be legal, but there's nothing else real about it. What difference does it make what cake I pick?

Livia isn't the only one here to taste cake. Will is here, too. It's the first time I've seen him since before Colin took me, and I look uncomfortably away, worrying that Colin's touch is some visible brand Will can see.

He holds his hands out to me and grips them, pulling

me toward him in the most awkward... I don't even know how to describe what he does so I'll just say it's awkward.

"Macy, finally! I told you the other day I could swing by and pick you up," he says.

I force a smile to my face and try not to shudder at his hands on mine. I want to cancel this wedding. I want to cancel this wedding. I want to cancel this wedding.

Then I start thinking maybe I could figure out a way to get Will to cancel the wedding instead. Would Colin punish me if Will was the one who canceled?

Will pulls out my chair and I sit, then the three of us start this bizarre rotation of cake tasting, passing the plates along in an assembly line of sugar gorging, and drinking black coffee in between bites.

"Oh, I do love the strawberry," Will says.

Truthfully I love it too, but I can't stand the idea of having this wonderful amazing cake with a man I don't love. Lately I can't even remember why we were friends in school. We have next to nothing in common but he seems oblivious to this as he guides the process along, cementing just another step in our ill-fated joining.

"Macy, what if we did alternating layers? We could have two layers of strawberry and then a layer of chocolate and yellow marble cake in the middle for guests to have an option. It would be like Neapolitan ice cream, but with cake." He is far too into this. I know it's customary for the groom to attend the cake tasting, but his interest in selecting wedding cake just convinces me further he's using me as some sort of beard.

I wonder if his family is super conservative, and that's why. I haven't met his family yet, which I realize is very strange, but they all live out of town and Will has such a busy work schedule. He isn't even going home for the holidays this year. Is there a reason he doesn't want his family to meet me? Or me to meet them? Would they not approve of me? Would they see through all this and know it's not real? Why did he even ask me to marry him? Maybe he wants kids too, and this seems like the normal way. I don't know anymore what's going on.

"Macy? Is that all right with you?" Will asks, indicating the two cake flavors.

I find myself nodding and going along with this selection, barely cognizant of the fact that Will and Livia just chose the wedding cake without any real input from me.

"I'd like hazelnut for the groom's cake," Will says.

I watch as he thumbs through the groom's cake design book. Livia shoots me a look behind his back. The look screams *If you don't end this sham wedding, I will!*

I ignore her and go back to studying Will. He's an architect and recently got a job at a firm here in the city though I'm not sure which one. He's kind of quiet about his work. He's quiet about a lot of things. His work. His family. He's like a shell with no person behind it, or like a movie extra with no backstory. His dark hair falls into his face as he looks at the groom's cakes.

I glance up at the baker and the employees who brought the sample cakes out. Surely they have to see this man and I are not in love. What must they think about this painfully awkward pairing before them?

My mind strays again for the millionth time to Colin's dark promises in my ear, his mouth on my neck, his hand between my legs, the way I came apart for him, the way he put me back together as quickly as he'd shattered me.

I force the thought from my mind and stop the tear before it slides down my cheek. I will not pine over a man who kidnapped me. Though am I more upset about the kidnapping or the abandonment... the fact that he set me free? I twist the bracelet around on my wrist. Not free. Electric fence. Unless it's a lie and it's just a bracelet. Unless I really am free except in my mind.

What if I'm the one who holds the key to my own cage? I push this thought away as quickly as it arises.

"I think this design for the groom's cake," Will says, pointing at a glossy photo. "What do you think, Macy?"

"Hmmm?"

"That was Soren's groom's cake," Livia says.

And she's right. The photo is a chocolate cake that looks like the art museum where Livia and Soren first met. But I can see why an architect would be drawn to it.

"I apologize," Will says formally. "I didn't realize."

"No, no, it's okay," Livia says. "You didn't know. If you want that cake, you should have it."

"Are you sure?"

Livia plasters on the fakest smile I've ever seen her face produce and nods like an overly happy robot.

"Well, okay, if you're sure." He nods to the baker to indicate that yes he will in fact have the exact same groom's cake that was featured at my best friend's wedding reception. I'm not sure this could be a bigger parody.

"Sorry," I mouth silently to her.

She just rolls her eyes and shrugs, though I know the eye roll isn't intended for me.

Then we look at the cake designs for the main wedding cake. I choose buttercream frosting and the first design I can find. I oooh and aaah over it and act like it's my dream cake just to make this confectionery nightmare end.

Will's chair scrapes out as he gets up and stretches his arms over his head. He's tall and despite his awkwardness he dresses sharply, like a man who understands clean lines and design. He has a kind face, kind eyes, a goofy sort of adorable smile.

"Macy, I'm afraid I've got to meet a client to do a walk-through of a building he wants redesigned."

He leans in and kisses me. It's just a brief peck on my lips, but I pull away as if burned. He smiles at me, seeming oblivious, and then leaves me with Livia.

I make the final arrangements with the baker and start to pay the deposit but she tells me she's already got Will's card details. I nod and Livia and I collect our things and go outside. I feel both grateful and guilty that Will seems to be picking up the tab for everything. His card mysteriously shows up to take care of each expense.

"Oh my god," Livia says as soon as we've gotten outside and she's checked to make sure Will isn't still within hearing distance. "I cannot deal with this bullshit wedding anymore. You can't marry him. You have to end it right the fuck now. Oh my god, that kiss. I need to bleach my eyeballs and take a shower from that kiss. He's so... cloying. Oh god."

Livia is beside herself. You'd think she was the one in this situation and not me.

"I want to do it," I say. I have to force these words out of my mouth because I one hundred percent do NOT want to do it, but I'm still holding out hope that Colin will show up and rescue-kidnap me before the wedding happens. And if he doesn't, I can still run on the wedding day. Because if he doesn't show up by then, he's not coming.

My mind screams at me for wanting a dangerous criminal to come kidnap me away from a wedding to a nice man who would give me a good life and be kind to me. Who the hell knows what awful things Colin would do to me?

A bolt of heat flares to life between my legs because my body knows exactly what kinds of things Colin would do to me.

"Why?" Livia laments. "Why do you want to marry him? You don't love him. You're not attracted to him. The way he touched you in there made my skin crawl. I cannot stand to watch this. I can't be a part of it! You deserve better than this. You deserve a man who will light you up inside. I don't understand why you're still doing this... why haven't you canceled already?"

"You know why. I want a baby, and I'm not getting any younger. I'm not going to find the right guy, Liv. If I was, I already would have found him."

Livia's hand moves over her belly almost imperceptibly. I stop for a moment to really observe her. I've been so wrapped up in my own dramas that I haven't *really* looked at my friend in a while. I notice her clothes aren't nearly as form fitting as they normally are. Her boobs look a little bigger...

"Liv...?"

She looks up with a guilty expression on her face, and I know she knows I've caught her. "Hmm?"

"Are you pregnant?"

She sighs. "I was waiting for the right time to tell people. I didn't want to steal the thunder of your fake wedding."

I can't even laugh at that because it's too tragic. "Whose is it?" There are after all three potential fathers.

She shrugs. "Soren insists it's his, but I don't think so. He couldn't make it to one of the doctor's appointments and I haven't told him yet... there are two heartbeats."

"Twins?" I ask stupidly, because of course it's twins. It's not like she's got an alien baby growing inside her, though that would definitely be a plot twist.

Livia nods. "Twins run in Dayne's family."

Dayne has always seemed like the most mysterious of the three. He has a quiet kind of power that's more calming than it is unnerving.

Livia's eyes widen suddenly. "Oh no you don't! You aren't

changing the subject. We were talking about the wedding and why you need to cancel it."

I've got to get her off this subject for good. I can't go through the next five months hearing this endless refrain, especially since we're ordering the invitations soon.

The only explanation I have for why I can't cancel the wedding, I can't tell her. Colin said not to. He said to keep doing everything just as I had done it. There's a twisted part of me that's afraid if I cancel the wedding he won't come for me. And that thought nearly breaks me because I shouldn't want him to come for me. Or maybe I'm afraid he'll punish me if I defy him. Is that a reasonable fear? I'm not sure. I'm not sure if it's reasonable to think the bracelet really is all he says it is either. I don't know what's reasonable anymore because all I have are my own crazed thoughts echoing around in my head and nobody to bounce them off of.

Maybe he got bored with me before he even got started. Maybe he gets off on ruining people's lives in petty ways— like lying about the bracelet and tricking me into going through with the wedding I don't want.

I'm not crazy or stupid. Probably. I don't want to be Colin's captive, but holy fuck, the way this man made me feel… the long wait for any man to make me feel that way…

Finally my mind surrenders, and I admit the grotesque truth. I want Colin to take me away from all this. I want to take the terrifying risk with a man who isn't safe because I'd rather feel more of what he made me feel than go my whole life feeling nothing at all.

Even as I think this, I know if he showed up I'd beg him not to take me, the fear of the very real situation would quickly edge out all the fantasy and desire.

"Macy!" Livia shouts.

"What?"

"It's like you're on another planet. Did you hear what I

said?"

I didn't, but I'm sure it was about why I shouldn't marry Will.

"It doesn't matter Liv. Look, people get divorced all the time. Will is a nice guy. He's got a stable situation. I'll marry him. I'll have a baby. I'll live a nice quiet safe life and if somehow the guy of my dreams shows up later, I'll get a divorce."

"Seriously?" Livia says, throwing her hands dramatically in the air.

It makes sense to me. I mean it's not like we live in a time in which I'm truly trapped in marriage once it happens. I'm not trapped. I can try it out, see how it goes, and if I'm miserable or find someone else later, I can leave. I feel like a terrible person even thinking this, but I don't think Will really wants me that much either. And anyway, how many people are resolutely serious when they say til death do us part?

The divorce rate would suggest not many. What people really mean is... being with my one true love for all of time is a really romantic notion but I deserve to be happy, so if I'm not in a few years we'll end it. Most people make the promise with good intentions, unable to see how unhappy they could become in just a few short years. The difference for me is I don't have that fairy tale mist hanging over me and my vows.

Livia finally sighs. "Fine. You know you can always stay in the guest wing at my place if things go south."

It's nearly five, and we still have an appointment with the florist. I've half convinced myself that it's actually reasonable to take Will's offer so I can shift myself into the next level of adulthood. He can be my starter husband if Colin doesn't come back. At this point I'm not sure which outcome would be worse.

# 11

## MACY

**F**ive Months Later.

I PACE in the makeshift dressing room inside the church. Colin never came back. It seems like it was a lifetime ago when I belonged to a terrifying and beautiful stranger for one day, and he made me feel things I didn't know were possible.

I stare down at the bracelet, more convinced than ever that it's not what he claimed it to be, that he's somehow just fucked with my head and ruined my life because that's what men like him do. Still, it seems such a petty form of evil for a man so all-encompassing.

There still lingers that other part of me that says something happened to him. That he's dead. He got in over his head with something and that's why he didn't come back and now I'm only moments away from my ill-fated wedding.

I met Will's family finally at the rehearsal dinner last

night. They seem like nice normal people who weren't overly concerned about the fact that they hadn't met me before because Will is quiet and keeps to himself. That's what they told me.

That statement of course has me worrying that maybe I got it all wrong. Maybe Will is a serial killer. Maybe that's why he needs a normal-looking life, so he can maintain a reasonable murder schedule. The more I think about that, the more I worry it's true. I need to run. Colin isn't coming. And it's crazy for me to want him to.

"Why aren't you dressed yet?"

I look up to find Livia wearing a light green dress. I ended up getting a few girls from the library to be brides-maids. Their dresses are off-white. Livia's is light green, to go with my darker green. We've almost entirely reversed all color expectations for this wedding.

Liv is about to pop out of her dress with the pregnancy. I swear she could have the babies five minutes ago; she's that pregnant. Of course I didn't know she was pregnant when I set this date, and she probably didn't know either.

There are close to a hundred guests out there. Will invited his whole big extended family, everybody he works with and some college friends. I invited Livia and her family and her men and people I work with. I'm not sure how we ended up with a hundred people, but with all the plus ones and everybody's kids, it adds up fast. At least I can have a normal-sized wedding cake without too much left over.

I'm not dressed yet because I'm still contemplating running—like literally running and fleeing the scene of my own wedding. But I can't do that to Will. I know I've treated him like a stranger these past several months, but we were pretty good friends in college. I actually do like this man. Just not that way.

I think that's why I said yes originally because it

somehow seemed less crazy in the moment. That is, until we went on several awkward dates and it became painfully clear to me what a mistake we were making. But we've both soldiered through, refusing to address the elephant in the room.

I finally unzip the garment bag holding my dress and have to fight back the gasp of surprise.

It's not my dark green dress. The dress in the bag is white.

"What is it?" Livia moves closer and she lets out the gasp I couldn't. "Oh my God. Where's your dress? How did this happen?"

I had last minute alterations and a final fitting last week. Maybe my dress got accidentally switched with someone else's. But even as I think it, I know that's not true.

It's Colin. It has to be Colin. He'd remarked on my dark green dress and how I should be married in white My heart thunders in my chest as I try to decide what to do.

"Macy?" Livia asks.

"I went back and got a white dress. I'm sorry. I lost my nerve with the dark green," I lie.

"Oh, honey. But you looked so great in that dress. I was so excited."

I shrug. "I know. But it's too late now. I have to wear the white."

"Did you want the dark green? Did you return it? Do you still have it? If you still have it I could go get it if you want. I mean they can't start the wedding without you."

"No, it's fine. I'll wear this. It's fine." But my hands are shaking as I run my fingers over the fine fabric.

"Do you need help getting dressed?"

I stare at her very pregnant belly knowing there isn't much she can do to help except maybe button some buttons.

If there are buttons. I don't even know what the dress looks like.

"I think I've got it," I say, not at all convinced any more by any of my many lies.

Colin is here. It's the only thought that will penetrate my brain right now. Colin is here. He's here. Is he going to take me before the wedding? Is he going to dramatically interrupt the wedding and take Will's place? No, that would be insane. You have to get a marriage license. That kind of thing just happens on soap operas.

But maybe he'll object and drag me away to the horror and gasps of the assembled guests.

I should run. I should run from both of them. I think I'm having a panic attack.

"Are you okay?" Livia asks.

My entire life has become one surreal reality show. How is this my life? How is any of this happening? It's been one innocuous decision after another leading to my doom. Accept an old friend's marriage proposal, what could possibly go wrong? Leave Soren alone with my tea, what could possibly go wrong? Keep planning the wedding I don't want, what could possibly go wrong?

Everything.

I shoo Livia out of the room so I can think. After about five minutes alone, I finally unzip the bag the rest of the way and free the dress from its protective casing.

*It's Colin. It's Colin. It's Colin.* My mind shrieks like a hyper-active candy-coated toddler.

It's a stunning gown—one I didn't see when I bought my dress. But that's not unusual because I didn't even look in the side of the store with the bigger designers. I knew I couldn't afford it and didn't want to fall in love with a dress I couldn't have.

I stare at the dress as though it might attack me and then

I continue to pace. I'm afraid to put the dress on and be taken by Colin, but I'm equally afraid to put the dress on and marry Will. Part of me doesn't want either fate.

I shake myself out of this craziness. There was a mix-up at the shop. Colin isn't coming. If he were coming he wouldn't wait until the very last second. He wouldn't wait until half an hour before I was getting married. Either he decided he didn't want me after all or something happened to him. And why do I care if something happened to him or if he doesn't want me? He's crazy and evil. He wanted to *own* me.

*For God's sake, get a grip!*

He talked about me like I was going to be presented on some altar to an angry volcano god.

I internally review my original stated plan. Marry the nice normal guy with the nice job and have a nice kid in a nice house. Life isn't a fairy tale. I know Livia got everything I wanted. I know there are men out there who could fulfill my fantasies if I had the courage to go out there and meet them, to try, to risk. But I don't have that kind of courage. My fantasies will remain safely tucked inside my head, and I will live the normal life fate dealt for me.

I take a few deep breaths and slip into the gown. It's silk and deceptively simple, a creamy soft white. The front hugs my curves as though it were made specially for me. The train is sort of bunched up or gathered in the back in a unique way that makes the gown look regal. And there is a veil. I said I wouldn't wear a veil. I said I wouldn't wear white, but I put it on anyway.

And now I am the antithesis of everything I said I would be.

I look down at the bracelet still on my wrist. How long am I going to wear it before I finally find some way to get it removed? Will hasn't asked about it. He probably hasn't even noticed it.

My dark red curls cascade around me as I pin the veil in place. The gown has a zipper so I don't need assistance. I stand in front of the mirror and just stare. Who is this woman? What is she about to do?

I should run. I should change out of this dress and run.

Before I can climb out a window, there's a knock on the door.

"Come in."

Livia's mouth drops open when she sees me. "Holy shit, Macy. You look beautiful."

I think I should be offended by her shock. But she's right. Normally I'm cute. Pretty maybe. But the glamorous woman in the mirror isn't Standard Macy by any stretch of the imagination.

I'm not wearing my glasses today, opting instead for contacts. My makeup is subtle but was professionally done along with my hair earlier in the day. My curls were relaxed around my face. I look like a glam 1940's Hollywood Starlet.

"Oh wow," Livia says again. "This is so much better than the green dress."

I hate to admit it, but it really is. It's the most beautiful dress I've ever seen in real life, and I'm wearing it.

Livia hands me my bouquet of soft white roses. Spring green shoots of filler flowers pop out around the edges. They match the gown exactly which seems so strange when I didn't plan it that way, but then white roses only come in so many shades and with a green dress what other color flowers was I going to carry? Then she grips my arm and guides me out of the room.

"Come on, the music is starting."

Before I know what's happening, the bridesmaids and Livia are halfway down the aisle. Then the music changes to the wedding march and everyone stands. I had momentarily considered Pachelbel's canon in D but Liv used that, and I really don't want to copycat her entire wedding even though that's the only other completely standard walk-down-the-aisle song aside from the one I'm actually walking down to.

Will looks slightly nervous standing at the front waiting for me. It's the first time he's seemed nervous or unsure this entire time. Maybe he does have feelings for me? But why? We have literally nothing in common and not even zero chemistry. We have negative chemistry.

My gaze keeps darting around looking for Colin. It's not like he can kidnap me out of the middle of a crowded church. How exactly would that go? And I realize of course that he can't object during that part of the ceremony. I mean he could but... he can't. Still I look for him, and a part of me is surprised he isn't here.

But most disturbing is realizing that some part of me really expected him to stop my wedding and that same part wanted it to happen. I need so much more therapy than I can afford.

The minister starts the ceremony, and it finally sinks in that I'm standing in front of a hundred people, my hands inside Will's hands, saying vows and exchanging rings and pledging to be together until one of us dies. Suddenly the flippant thoughts of leaving if it doesn't work out seem much more difficult, as though wedding vows were some sort of magic binding me unwillingly to this man I don't love or even want to sleep with.

This is a great time for me to be realizing I don't want to sleep with the man I just randomly decided was going to father my children. And if I didn't have the strength of will to run away from this wedding to begin with or cancel it at any point, how will I find the will to leave and end it? By the time I've worked through all this the minister is to the point about objecting.

No voice rises to save me. I want to object, but of course I don't. I just stand there numbly allowing this nightmare to continue, making no move to save myself from this lackluster fate. I'm so angry at myself right now, for just allowing this to happen without stopping it. I should have stopped it before now. Fuck what Colin said. Who the fuck is he? I should have canceled the wedding.

Finally the minister pronounces us man and wife, and Will and I share a kiss as clumsy and painful to watch as the few others that have preceded it. We are announced as a couple, the music starts, and we go back up the aisle past smiling faces.

When we get outside in the bright sunlight, Will is smiling, too. He seems actually happy about this. "Well, we did it. We're married," he says.

"Yay," I say, and it's such a fake yay I don't know how the hell he doesn't hear it.

The rest of the day goes by in a blur. First it's about a million photos before the reception. By the time we get to the party, it's already in full swing. Then I'm confronted with every single person Will has ever met. I listen for a good two hours as person after person says Will and I are just perfect for each other and they knew he would find the right girl someday. Everyone is welcoming me to the family, and I feel like the worst person who ever existed.

Our first dance is a slow song without any fancy choreography. I eat at our table while Will is distracted talking to some people I think he works with.

"How do you feel?" Livia whispers, slipping into a chair next to me.

"Like I might vomit," I say.

She looks extremely worried, and I realize maybe I

shouldn't have been so honest. After all I haven't bothered with honesty for months now. My best friend doesn't even know I was kidnapped. I glance over to the table Livia was sitting at. Soren's dark gaze is trained on me.

I wish I knew what he was thinking. I wonder if he knows something about Colin. But there's no way I'll ask him. How would that conversation even go? *Hey you know the guy you gave me to? Well he let me go temporarily and said he'd come back. Haven't heard from him and just wondered if maybe he died because I really don't want to be married to this other guy and I can't stop touching myself thinking about the man you gave me to.*

I look away from Soren, and finally, after several long minutes I feel his hard gaze leave me, and I can breathe freely again.

"Where are you two going on your honeymoon?" one of Will's cousins asks.

"I'm taking her all over Europe. To England, Ireland, Scotland, Spain, Italy..."

"How will you fit that all into a week?" she asks.

"It's not going to be a week. My firm is sending me on some work assignments overseas, so it's a working honeymoon. We'll be gone a month."

"Oh wow. Macy, what about your work?"

"Oh, I got a leave of absence," I say.

I've only known about this honeymoon plan for the past two months, but I'd convinced myself it would give us some time to get to know each other.

"Well that's lucky!" she says. "I'm so jealous. I'd love to go to Europe for a month."

I smile politely, biting back the urge to offer her my ticket and crawl under the table.

We cut the cake next, and I get to have some of that nearly magical strawberry cake. Will's family goads him to smash it on my face because that's what you do, but Will is a perfect gentleman.

I somehow survive the garter experience and more of Will's fumbling while everybody laughs and cheers, and then I toss the bouquet. The reception finally winds down and we leave through a tunnel of sparklers to a limousine that takes us to a nearby hotel.

"I can't wait to get to the room," Will says once we're alone in the limo.

I shrug away from his kiss. "I'm kind of tired after today," I say.

"Well, it is our wedding night. I was very patient with you."

Alarm bells start to go off but then he laughs and says, "I'm kidding. You should see your face. Yeah I'm tired too."

If anything this *joke* raises even more alarm bells because it doesn't feel like a joke. He seems very different all of a sudden from the person I thought he was.

My heart pounds against my chest as he leads me to the third floor and down the hallway to the honeymoon suite. What do I really know about this man? Aside from being casual friends in college, I mean. He slips his key card into the door. A silent beep and a flick to green. Then he opens the door, picks me up, and carries me over the threshold.

He sets me on my feet and shuts the door behind him. There's champagne and chocolate and strawberries on a tray on the bed which is covered in red rose petals. Candles are lit around the room. There's a fire roaring in the fireplace. And even though it's March, the fire is welcome because it's still very cold outside. The bathroom door opens, and a man in a suit steps out drying his hands on a towel.

I shriek, shocked that someone else would be here, but then I look into his face and my heart nearly stops.

*Colin.*

I expect Will to demand to know who this man is and what he's doing in our room. But instead he says, "Sir, your toy. You've got her free and clear with nobody missing her for the next month."

I gasp and spin to find Will blocking my exit.

"Will? What are you doing?"

He rolls his eyes. "Oh please. Anybody could see you didn't really want to marry me. Imagine if I'd wanted to marry you. You would have dragged me through a loveless marriage. Really, Macy, I kind of think you deserve this if we're being honest. You could have canceled the wedding at any time."

I turn back to find Colin smirking... "What? Why? I... what?" I really can't form coherent words or thoughts right now nor can I figure out how this is even happening.

How does Colin know Will? How is Will working for Colin? What is happening right now?

Colin just smiles. "William has been working for me."

"But, what if I'd canceled the wedding?"

Colin shrugs, seemingly unconcerned. "I had contingency plans, but you would have been punished for disobeying me."

"But... what about Will's family? Aren't they going to ask questions when I just never show up again? Holidays are a thing."

"Are you sure that was *really* his family?"

I'm gaping at him now. I mean the more explanation I get the less real it sounds. I'm trying desperately to make this make sense. But even if both Will and Colin said "Gotcha!" it still wouldn't make sense.

"Who the hell else would they be?" I ask. I feel the more I allow myself to be pulled along into this insane alternate reality the more pieces of my otherwise sound mind are drifting away from me.

"Actors. They think they're part of a sort of hidden camera reality show. And they all signed NDAs about it because of supposed rules with the studio. They think this is a pilot episode and may not make it onto TV. So when it doesn't, they'll just shrug and move on with their lives."

"You said you had me for a month free and clear. What happens after a month?"

"By then you'll belong to me so completely that you won't want to get away. Right now only your body is mine. But soon your soul and mind will belong to me as well."

He says this as though he's collecting baseball cards. As if all these pieces of me will at some point be put in a display case for guests to ooh and aah over.

I should be offended, but my body only has one setting with this man: turned on. Seriously how did I even survive on this planet this long? My libido obviously wants me dead.

"Here are the papers," Will says, pulling a manila folder out of his tuxedo jacket. "I took them off the minister when he wasn't paying attention."

Colin takes the papers out, studies them, then tosses them in the fire. "Congratulations on your divorce, Macy. No legal filed paperwork, no legal marriage."

# 12

## COLIN

S ix months prior.

I STAND OVER MACY, feeling quite satisfied with myself when Jeffrey interrupts with a phone call. Fucking Soren. I could strangle that motherfucker. He has the worst timing. I take the phone out into the hallway.

"What is it?" I growl.

"I spoke to Dayne about your request."

"And?"

"You can come back to the club, use his cottage, and have the collar under one condition."

"And that condition would be...?" Soren is the most infuriating person I know. What? Does he want me to beg him for information? Perform tricks like a circus monkey? He just doles information out like breadcrumbs in the forest that I'm supposed to happily scoop up and put in a basket like some frolicking Red Riding Hood.

He forgets I'm also a wolf.

"A sacrifice," is Soren's cryptic reply.

"What in the fuck does that mean?" He's twisting things around on me. Macy was payment.

"And there's one other condition. She has to remain untouched. We want a *virgin* sacrifice," he says.

"You couldn't have told me that before you brought her to me? I could have just kept her under surveillance with Will."

"We hadn't decided our terms yet. So you've already fucked her?"

*Already?* I've had her for nearly twenty-four hours. I *should* have already done it. And I'm still not quite sure why I held back.

"No. Went down on her," I say. What I really want to do is accuse Soren of knowing exactly what he's doing, setting me up so I can't meet the requirements of his offer.

"Anything else?" Soren asks, his tone deceptively calm.

"No." I want to kill him. Who the fuck is he to control what I do with the woman he *gave* me? Has he forgotten how this all started and who has the power? Who *had* the power. Now that it's something I want that he has, I'm no longer the one calling the shots. It's just like that miserable bastard to flip things around again so somehow he's the one in control of everything.

"Colin?" Soren says like I just hung up.

He knows what I'm thinking... the complicated calculus running through my head, trying to decide if it's a win or a lose for me. He'd be running the same calculations through his head if our positions were reversed. He probably ran them when he offered me Macy to begin with.

"You're getting something you want, too," Soren says. "Doesn't that make it a win-win. And nothing changes the fact that she's yours. Come to Costa Rica. We're all at The

Cottage. Meet with us. You can pick who will be involved. We have a list of members for you to select from, but we can't discuss the details over the phone. You know where to meet. Tomorrow night, nine o'clock."

"I can't just leave Macy here alone with Jeffrey, you know how he is. I can't guarantee purity if I do."

"I'm sure you'll think of something." Soren disconnects the call.

Fuck. Fuck. Fuck.

I haven't wired Will's money yet. I could sweeten the deal and keep him on Macy for a bit longer. But I can't let her out of my sight without at least a tracker.

I had the bracelet made, knowing I'd need to monitor her when I first let her resume her life more-or-less. I can't keep my wife under lock and key, after all. So, I can test the leash.

I don't know. Maybe I should just let her go. She's already getting inside my head.

Jeffrey has been lurking within earshot since we got out into the hallway. I turn to him now. "Pack my bags. I need to be in the air in two hours."

"And the girl?"

"I'll handle the girl." Maybe this is for the best. Maybe with enough space and distance from her, I'll come to my senses. Maybe I won't return for her at all.

# 13

## COLIN

T*he Present*

MACY LOOKS like she may go into shock. As soon as Soren returned from his honeymoon, he gave me a dossier on her and told me his terms. I was intrigued but not quite ready to collect or commit. At the same time I was paranoid she'd meet someone while I was making up my mind. Ordinarily that wouldn't be a problem, I could arrange something. I could have her no matter who entered her life. But I got caught up in this virgin sacrifice idea. When Soren first used those words with me, something dark and primal kicked in.

Since that time, it has been brought to my attention that Macy is a kinky little thing. How one woman can be simultaneously so innocent and so filthy is anybody's guess.

I couldn't have anybody deflowering her before I was ready for her. And so the deep dive into her past commenced as I tried to figure out who I could bring on board with my plans. Who could I get to babysit and guard her virtue?

As it turned out there was a man from her past who had a lot of debts which I could make go away. When I interviewed him and discovered he'd actually made one of these *if we're both single by thirty* pacts, I knew Macy was a gift from the universe—or more likely some particularly dark god who just liked my style. Synchronicity like that doesn't just happen. I couldn't have planned for it. But it was a perfect set-up.

"That will be all, William," I say, dismissing him finally. He's been standing here leering at my prize as though I'm going to let him in on the action. While I like to share, I wouldn't share her with this guy. I know she doesn't want him and sharing is as much about her pleasure as it is about my power to do so.

When he doesn't move, I say, "The money has been wired. Remember my terms."

He nods and leaves.

William won't talk. He knows what will happen if he does. Plus, he participated in the crime, and he knows I have evidence to that effect.

Macy backs away, fumbling for the doorknob.

"Do you like the dress?" I ask.

"W-what?"

This clearly isn't what she expected me to say. "The dress? Do you like it?"

She looks down as if she's forgotten what she's even wearing. Her hands skim over the smooth silk. This one dress costs more than Macy makes in a year. I saw it live on a runway. I'm not ordinarily the type of man who goes to a bridal couture runway show, but I had business with the designer. I happened to look up, saw the dress, and claimed it for Macy. It's one-of-a-kind. Just like her.

This girl was absolutely not going to wear a green wedding dress.

"It's beautiful." Then she looks up at me, and there are tears in her eyes. "I thought you were going to stop the wedding. Why didn't you?"

Now it's my turn to be shocked. She was waiting for me to come for her? I stand still for a full minute while my brain goes completely offline as I try to grasp the fact that she was waiting to be rescued from this wedding... by me of all people.

In truth, once I met her in person I'd meant what I said. I did want to trade Will out and marry her. I wanted to rewrite my entire carefully crafted plan. Not a legal marriage, of course... but I wanted to be the one standing at the front of the church reciting vows. The fact that I wanted this—even fleetingly—still disturbs me.

But then I remembered Livia was present when Soren first promised Macy to me, and she'd likely put two and two together. Then Soren called, demanding my presence at the club.

"I just wanted the dream wedding. Like Livia," she says, and the sadness in her voice is palpable.

"Wasn't it the dream? You got all the things you wanted."

She thinks much of her wedding was financed through Livia by Soren and that other things were favors and lucky breaks and discounts. But behind the scenes I was the one signing all the checks. Metaphorically, of course. Nobody still writes checks. I used my black card.

She just looks at me like I'm the stupidest human who ever existed. "No! It's not the dream. It wasn't what I wanted. I wanted..." She trails off as though she's already said too much. And she has. Somehow I know what she was going to say. Maybe not in these words, but she didn't want the wedding. That's not the fairy tale. The fairy tale is the perfect wedding to the man she wants.

And somehow, she wanted me. *Who* is this creature? How does she exist in the world?

She holds up the bracelet. "Is this even real? Or is it just another trick?"

I capture and hold her gaze in mine. "I heard every. Single. Orgasm. Were you thinking about me while you had them?"

She blushes furiously and looks away. That's a yes.

I loosen my tie and take two strides toward her. She flinches as though I'm going to hit her.

"You got all the things you wanted, Macy. Just not all in one package."

She shakes her head stubbornly, the tears still moving down her face. "No. I wanted a man who loves me."

I freeze. It's like she knows this is the one thing I'm not sure I'm capable of giving someone. I can give her luxury, comfort, safety—from everyone but me at least—pleasure, kink. I can buy her anything she wants, but I don't even know if I have a heart to give. And I don't trust anyone, including myself.

I push her up against the door, my hand wrapped around her throat. Any other sane human would struggle at this point, but her body melts against mine as though my hands on her could never be bad in any context. And I find it still unnerves me. I don't know what to do with this level of trust aimed at me.

"No," I say, "That's not your fairy tale. You don't want some boring sweet vanilla man like William to ride in on a horse and take you off to a normal happily ever after in the suburbs with a minivan. You want the fire that burns you, the storm that consumes you and sweeps you out to sea far from any hope of rescue. Wish. Granted."

Before she can respond, there's a knock on the door. "Mr. Black?"

Right on time. I stand back and level a hard look at Macy. "My attorney is as ruthless as I am and, much like me, he considers laws little more than options to consider. You *will* sign the papers."

# 14

## MACY

Colin's words about the fire and the storm and the sea ignite something in me. Am I this transparent? My dangerous desires are going to get me killed. He is not safe. He's made this explicitly clear, and yet even if it were real with William, I didn't want him or that boring safe life. That's the problem with safe... it's also boring.

I've been rescued from boredom and thrown into uncertainty with a man who lights me up even as I know I can never trust him. I jump as a knock reverberates against my back.

"Mr. Black?" a male voice says from the other side of the door.

Colin gives me some breathing room and the look he sends me has my heart fluttering in my chest. I'm not sure what this look is meant to convey. It could be some kind of warning, or a promise for what he has planned later after this interruption has gone away.

"My attorney is as ruthless as I am and, much like me, he considers laws little more than options to consider. You *will* sign the papers."

I just stare blankly at Colin like a little idiot.

What papers? But then I remember breakfast the morning after I was given to him when he showed me the legal documents and how he needed a "Mrs. Black."

I'd been full of tea, flaky buttery croissants, and bravado. I can't seem to find any of that bravado right now. I mean there's still a tracking and surveillance bracelet around my wrist. And he's set up this entire insane scenario. I still can't wrap my mind around the fact that Will was working for him. This whole time. He never would have contacted me about that stupid pact otherwise.

And that kind of hurts my feelings a little bit. But I can't start crying about it now because that would be ridiculous with everything else going on.

Maybe Will and I weren't that great of friends in college. And we were sort of drunk that night when we made the pact. But still. How did Colin find out about that? How did he know he could get Will to turn on me for some money? How much did he pay him to go along with all of this?

It occurs to me suddenly that maybe Will had liked me back in college, that maybe he'd wanted more than friendship but either I didn't see it or didn't want to see it. So was this some kind of payback because I couldn't call forth those feelings from the romance aether?

I move out of the way as Colin opens the door to invite his attorney inside. The man gives me a long, slow once-over that gives me the creeps.

"She's off limits," Colin says.

So that wasn't my imagination. I'm reassured at least in this moment that nothing seems to get past Colin, and he's veto'd whatever desires were in the attorney's gaze.

The attorney doesn't comment on this, but he does stop leering at me. Suddenly he's all professionalism. The three of us sit at a table in the living area part of the honeymoon suite. The papers are passed to Colin. He skims over them as if making sure everything is in order and signs them, then the papers are slid to me along with a blue ballpoint pen. Two expectant gazes land on me.

"Sign," Colin orders.

"I-I need to read them to know what I'm signing," I say.

"This isn't a negotiation. It doesn't matter what they say. You're signing them. They're for your benefit."

There's no reaction to Colin's coercion from the attorney. It's super nice to know we have such ethical people working in law.

"If they're for my benefit I should be able to read them." I fight not to flinch as I say these words. Sometimes I can be very stubborn, and my anger is about to edge out my fear. Maybe.

The attorney raises a brow. "You've got your work cut out for you training this one," he says. And the leer is back again.

"Oh, she will bend to me," Colin says, sounding supremely confident.

He's probably right. That growl in his voice just now? Oh, I felt that in places I shouldn't feel it.

I feel the blush rise to my face so I look down at the papers. I'm hoping the boring legalese will douse the flames of these feelings because I don't want Colin or his creep attorney to be able to figure out that I'm turned on right now. There are about a thousand ways that could go badly for me.

I know realistically I'm not getting out of this room until I've signed these papers and that Colin possibly is never letting me go anyway. And didn't I spend months fantasizing about him? Didn't I spend months hoping he'd rescue me from this farce of a wedding?

But still, I want to know what I'm signing, and unless he

plans to murder me right here right now or punish me in front of the attorney, I'm not signing until I know. Oh my god... why did I just think that? His attorney is a slime ball, but still, somehow the idea of him watching Colin turn me over his knee and spank me in front of him excites me.

"Just sign," Colin says interrupting my crazy mental babbling.

It takes me a whole five seconds to work up the nerve to stop pretending to read and look up. I stare at Colin. "You waited months. You can wait fifteen minutes while I read."

He actually laughs at this. "By all means, Mrs. Black. Read, then."

And so I read. If I leave I get nothing. If I leave after children, he gets custody but I get very generous terms around seeing my own kids. How magnanimous. We both know he's not letting me go anywhere so that's just for show so no red flags get triggered when the paperwork gets filed. I'm not sure how this could be legally enforcible anyway. It seems so one-sided.

Except the children are referred to as heirs—heirs which I'm contractually obligated to deliver to him. Like a brood-mare. This is what I imagine pre-nups for royal weddings look like. Yes, I've done all that background research too. There is this totally creepy level of fertility checking and demands of doing one's duty to produce royal babies. And while officially this offends all my modern sensibilities, on another secret level I don't like to think about, this idea turns me on. A lot. My spank bank fantasies could fill a library, and a lot of them are in the *breeding an heir* category. Don't judge me.

I'm not marrying into a royal family, but I may as well be. Colin has an enormous amount of money and power.

On paper he really is the dream. But I also get this

distressing vibe that he's murdered people, so that takes the shine off things just a little.

If he leaves me, very generous terms provide for my safety and comfort. It is *lavish*. I mean there are specifications about properties I will be given and sums of money so big I can barely comprehend it. I even get staff, like people to drive me around and guard me, even personal shoppers for things like grocery shopping which apparently wealthy people never do for themselves... unless they like doing it, of course. If he can afford to give me all this if he leaves, then how much must he actually *have*?

There isn't even some no-cheating stipulation, just, if he leaves me, here is the long list of extravagant shit I get. You'd think he'd *want* me to read these papers, since it makes him almost look like a human being, instead of a man posing as a god, accepting me as tribute.

"Do they meet with your approval, Mrs. Black? Would you like a larger palace in the event I take your virtue, get bored, and toss you to the curb?"

I don't respond to his goading, I just sign. The reality is... I don't need his money. Sure, it might make certain aspects of my life more comfortable but if I had the freedom to leave and did so, the *you get nothing* threat, really just doesn't land with me. *We're not all gold diggers, asshole.*

The attorney puts the papers in a briefcase, gives Colin a copy, and then leaves me alone with my generous captor. Colin slides the deadbolt into place, then turns to me.

I stand, totally still, a deer frozen in front of the oncoming car as he stalks me. He stops a couple of feet away.

"Take off the ring."

"W-what?"

"The ring. Remove it."

I glance down at my shaking hand, already having forgotten the shiny gold wedding band.

"But... I signed those papers and... don't you want me to wear a ring?" Maybe he wants me to wear a ring he picked, instead of William's ring. But if Will was working for him this whole time, wouldn't the ring really be Colin's? He no doubt paid for it.

I take the ring off and offer it to Colin.

He shakes his head. "No, read the inscription."

It never occurred to me that the ring would have something engraved inside the band. It's not the kind of thing Will and I talked about. I cross the room to a floor lamp and hold the ring under the light as I examine the engraved inscription.

In harsh block font, the words read: "Mrs. Colin Black."

An involuntary shiver runs down my spine, as goosebumps pebble out across my exposed arms. I thought I was saying vows to Will, but the ring slipped on my finger shows me belonging to another man entirely. It feels as though some kind of dark magic swirled around as I was tricked, sealing my fate to Colin, even as I thought I was marrying someone else.

I'm not sure what to say to this or how to react, so I start to put the ring back on.

"Give it to me," he says, holding his hand out.

So the ring was just him making a point about how foolish I am? How easily he can move me across his game board into whatever strategic position he wants me in?

But I don't argue. I can't bring myself to argue to wear his ring, a ring that brands me as his and basically has a "property of" sticker on it, in case anybody gets confused about ownership rights. I pass the gleaming ring to him, and he slips it into his pocket.

"Don't worry, Mrs. Black. You'll get it back at the appropriate time, but I should be the one to put it on you. I want the moment to have... gravity."

My mouth is dry as I stare at him. I feel so awkward. What now? I'm caught off guard by his next words because they're so normal.

"You picked over your food at the reception. Would you like me to order you something?"

I don't know what I expected to happen when we were alone again, but it wasn't for him to order me room service.

"Um... yes?" And suddenly I find I can't meet his gaze. I don't know why I'm like this. One minute I'm all bravado and defiance and staring people down, and the next I am so unbelievably shy that it's painful to even have his gaze on me.

"Yes, what?"

I stare at the upholstery of the sofa. I know what he wants. It's been a while since I was alone with him. But I played and replayed that day over and over in my mind for months. I touched myself thinking about it so many times I lost count... all while going along with the engagement to William. But the shyness comes over me again and... I just can't say the word.

There's a long silence—a silence that stretches before me like an infinite dark forest.

I yelp when his hand is suddenly wrapped around my arm and he drags me back to the chair I'd sat in to sign the papers.

"Don't move," he says.

I watch as he crosses the room and pulls out a black case. He removes something—I can't determine what—and strides back across the floor to me. I shrink back. There is resolute purpose in his gaze, and I want to blurt out "Master", but I can't force the word out.

Because I'm me, and I like to make things harder than

they need to be. It's clear to me when I'm using the intelligence I supposedly have that this man will not be denied. He has seemingly infinite resources and just managed to set up a situation where I won't be missed for a month. I don't want to think about the implications of that.

He ties my wrists behind my back with black rope and gags me. It's a ball gag which I can tell came from some super high-end kink store because the leather straps are soft. The ball isn't too big. The way it fits is actually... comfortable? I know that sounds weird, but it's not a distressing feeling. At least not physically. I'm a little bit distressed mentally over the fact that I'm not screaming or fighting him.

He bends so he's eye level with me. "You won't speak again until you're ready to say it."

Then he crosses to the phone and orders us some food like all of this is just a normal day for him. When he gets off the phone he sits on the sofa and pulls out some papers and a laptop and starts doing some work. I have no idea what kind of work because I don't know what he does, but he's very engrossed in it, whatever it is.

I have time while we wait for the food to think about my predicament. I still don't fully understand why this man is doing all of this. I mean surely he could get any woman he wanted. Even if his social skills are lacking, he's rich and hot and commanding, and that opens the legs of probably eighty percent of the female population all by itself. Maybe he's already fucked all of those women.

And if he doesn't want to be bothered with relationships, he could pay for sex. Hell, he could pay for this *stockholder-pleasing Mrs. Black* he claims to need. It could be a business arrangement instead of a felony. I think about the papers I signed. Did Soren read these papers and approve them? Are these the terms Soren secured for me?

Am I supposed to feel grateful about this?

# 15

## COLIN

I'm pretending to work because I'm suddenly a teenage boy with a raging hard on and a crush. This is so fucking ridiculous. I need to punish this girl for all the things she makes me feel. She watches me, and I watch her. Predator and prey. But I swear a fucked-up part of me thinks I may be the prey. I just don't buy Macy's innocent act.

I know she's a virgin, so there is a sense in which she's innocent, but I can't make any sense out of her reactions to anything. That first night when Soren delivered her to me... all that made sense. And on some level her coming apart under my attentions made sense. But right now she isn't making sense. She's not fighting or struggling or crying or whimpering. Is she in some kind of shock?

I have no idea.

Within a month I'm sure I won't have to worry about letting her off the leash. I'm half not worried about it now, considering what a good girl she was while she was away from me. She didn't try to run. She didn't try to remove the bracelet. And those sweet moans almost-but-not-quite cloaked by the shower spray... then the moans later when she was in bed each night and every morning... yes... my Macy is a very good girl.

I'm the one acting like the virgin. Hundreds of women have been in my bed. They've knelt for me, crawled for me, sucked my cock, swallowed, bared their asses for their spankings... all of it. Most of it was an act. But they did these things. And I'm about to be taken down by this... freckle-faced, red-haired... virgin with impossibly innocent green eyes along with that unexpected fire that intrigues me.

My internal insanity is interrupted by a knock on the door. Room service. I ordered for Macy since she was in no position to tell me what she wanted. Maybe she should have followed my rules.

Macy's eyes widen as I cross to the door. I'm curious about what she'll do. I could inform her that I could have the person delivering the food killed or that I could kill him myself. Both things are true. But I don't want to influence her reaction. I want to see what she'll do without any input from me.

I open the door to allow the food to be rolled in. The man—really kid... he's about twenty—stops cold when he sees Macy. She sits there, bound and gagged in her wedding dress at the table. Her pale green eyes are wide, and her face is flushed. I'm just now noticing the way her wrists are tied back combined with the dress she's wearing, pushes her breasts up in the most inviting way.

It's a testament to how much she's messing with my mind that I'm only now noticing this.

The guy stares at her tits, and I know he can't decide if he's walked in on a hostage situation or a sex game. The hard on he's sporting suggests he thinks probably the latter. It's a reasonable deduction. She is, after all, wearing a wedding dress in the honeymoon suite, and I'm not behaving in the sneaky way of a kidnapper.

"You can put the food on the table," I say, still watching them both with interest.

I am fascinated. Macy has this small golden opportunity to struggle or cry or make any sort of distressed sound to alert this guy to the fact that she's in trouble. But she's smart.

And she seems to understand implicitly that remaining calm will keep the kid alive.

"Y-yes, Sir," he says.

I arch an eyebrow at the title and look at Macy. I'm sure she understands that look... like... See? He can give me a title. Why not you? I admit Master is a different thing than Sir, though both indicate that someone is above you in some sort of power hierarchy. Still, Master is the more objectifying title. For her, not me.

He puts the food on the table, barely able to tear his gaze from Macy's tits.

"Would you like to stay and watch me deflower her?" I ask. She won't be deflowered until Costa Rica, so this kid isn't seeing shit, but I'm enjoying this show.

He flushes brighter red than Macy if that's even possible. "N-no, Sir. I... I have work."

I laugh at this and turn my attention back to my sort-of bride. Wait... is she turned on right now? Her pupils are dilated, and her breathing is coming out in a way that in any other circumstance would suggest to me a woman ready to come.

I pull out a roll of hundreds and press them into his hand. "Nobody likes a gossip," I say.

"N-No Sir."

He scurries out of the room like he's on fire. As soon as I shut the door I pick up my cell phone and dial my guard at the end of the hallway. "Follow and stay on that guy. Let me know if he talks to anyone."

I hear the obligatory *Yes, Sir* before the call disconnects, and I turn my attention back to Macy.

I'm not too worried about the kid. I'm registered under an alias. Someone else signed in for me. I kept to back entrances. No cameras have caught me. This whole suite was swept for electronic bugging and cameras before I entered. And no fingerprints will be left behind. It's all very... clean.

I sit at the table across from my captive and remove the silver lid from my steak and baked potato. I leave Macy's covered for now.

"Are you ready to give me a title?" I ask conversationally as I cut into the steak.

She watches me for a minute as if weighing her options.

"I'll feed you either way," I say. I may be a bastard but I'm not going to starve her. She needs to know she's more-or-less safe with me, and I won't withhold any basic needs. That doesn't mean there won't be punishments for all of these infractions. I'm keeping a list.

And of course she tests me by shaking her head no.

I sigh and take a bite. It's medium rare and perfect. The guys in the kitchen know how to make a steak.

"Why not?"

She can't give me a real answer, she's still gagged. And I love the way she looks now. Gags aren't a big fetish for me, but I realized it might be necessary with her. I didn't know if she'd start screaming and make a scene. I could have had her delivered directly to the jet, but I wanted to sleep on the ground tonight. Although the jet has a large and very comfortable bed, I'm not the biggest fan of air sleep. I'm not great with flying, though I mask my anxiety well. After all, I would hardly inspire terror in people if they knew I was a nervous flyer.

She just shrugs.

I finish my dinner and drink down the glass of cold water that came with it. Ordinarily I'd have something a bit stiffer than water, but I want to maintain a level head.

I motion her forward, and she looks confused at first but finally figures out what I want and bends forward so I can remove the gag. When it's gone I press a glass of water to her lips and allow her to drink.

"Are you going to untie me?" she asks.

"Are you going to address me?" I counter.

"I can't. It's weird."

But the blush on her face tells a different story.

"It gets weirder the longer you resist it."

She seems to consider the truth of this. I take the lid off her food and cut her steak.

"Are you fucking kidding me?" she asks.

"Language," I say, as if I'm chastising a toddler. I hold a piece of the meat up to her mouth.

She considers me. "Am I going to survive you?"

"Most likely."

I prod at her lips with the steak, and finally she relents to let me feed her.

# 16

# MACY

I can't believe I'm letting this man feed me like a small child. This steak is amazing though. It's taking everything in me not to rattle on about Angus beef and inform Colin about all the random weird facts I happen to know about it. Also, this meat was pasture-raised. I can tell. Factory farmed meat is the worst. Even aside from the animal cruelty, it just tastes bad. If you're going to eat meat, it's important that your food eats good food, too.

*Letting him feed me* is probably strong terminology. It's not like I have a lot of choices here. But he's not starving me or beating me. And I know that's in him. That potential. I didn't just imagine it the first time when Soren took me to his estate. This man is dangerous. He has a wicked looking scar above his left eye that seems to underline this point. It doesn't detract from his beauty... but it does give one pause.

Did he get into a knife fight? Did someone try to assassinate him? Is he in a position where his death would be called assassination?

I honestly don't know why I'm resisting calling him what he wants to be called. I don't know why I'm pushing him.

There is this deeply fucked-up part of me that desperately wants to be his good girl and do whatever pleases him. But there is another part of me that wants to find out what happens when I say no. How will he react? How safe am I ultimately with this man?

You don't know how safe you are with a man until you tell him no.

And I know that's stupid, because if I'm not safe—and why would I be safe?—goading him into... punishing me... It could put me in a lot of danger. But he's being very calm about all this.

As he's feeding me the baked potato I also have to really fight to not tell him why restaurant baked potatoes are so different from how people normally make them at home.

What they do is they drizzle them with olive oil and salt and pepper the skins before wrapping them in the foil to bake. Some of the oil bakes into the potato which is what makes them fall apart and taste so great. But I don't say this. I'm still mortified I rambled about the difference in fine and bone china the last time he had me. Like he cares.

And part of me is afraid if I let too much of my Encyclopedic weirdness out that he'll get tired of it, and me, and that it won't be safe for me. I'm not sure I believe in that contract I signed, that he'd just let me go and give me the fairy tale without the prince. Like a Barbie Dream House... Ken not included.

He doesn't push me again about the title. I don't think he's given up this battle, he's just choosing not to do anything about it right now. Maybe because we're in a hotel —not tucked away at his private compound—and if I scream, someone might hear.

I'm not sure why I haven't screamed.

He unties me and guides me into the bedroom part of the suite. Okay, this is happening. This is happening right now. I'm about to be deflowered on my fake wedding night by a man who basically somehow owns me, and I want him even though I shouldn't but... I can't just...

"C-Colin?" My voice comes out small, but he heard me.

He comes up behind me, pulling me flush against him. I feel his hard erection press against my lower back through the silk of my dress. His hand wraps around my throat as he pulls me closer.

"What did you call me?" he whispers in my ear.

And suddenly I'm so overloaded with so many feelings and sensations. Terror, arousal... safety. I know that last one doesn't make sense at all, but when his hands are on me... it's how I feel. I don't understand it but when he touches me like this I know he would protect me from anything. And I don't know how I know it or why I know it. But it comes from my *knower*. You know, that part of you that just knows things? It's not logical. I can't break it down with charts. It's not even my feelings... it's not emotional. It's just... I know.

A breathy sigh leaves my throat as my body melts and surrenders against his.

"I'm sorry, Master." The resistance has left me now because when he touches me like this, I feel too much his to call him anything else. The word that before felt silly and out of context and embarrassing, seems like the most normal thing in the world to call him when he unleashes this side of himself. That ruthless storm. Like Soren. I can't resist that energy. I feel the same things with Colin as I felt around Soren, which both relieves me and repulses me.

It relieves me because these feelings aren't directed at my best friend's husband. And it repulses me because Colin isn't playing a kinky game. I am *actually* his property. I'm trying hard to hold on to rage and indignance and offense about this but I just want him to take me and finally rip away this barrier to all the desires that have been kept locked within me for far longer than is normal.

He spins me to face him.

"Good girl," he says. Then his hand is around the back of my neck, his fingers threading into my hair as he pulls me in for one of those kisses only he can make real. I know I have practically no experience, but I've kissed men, and the way Colin kisses is... it's like he literally needs his mouth on mine for survival.

These desperate mewling whimpers are coming out of me. He turns me away from him again and unzips the dress. I don't want to take it off. I want to wear it forever because there will never be another day in my life when I can wear this perfect dress. It's the softest, smoothest silk. So much stronger than it looks. It should be delicate and breakable, but it's strong.

I will not start talking about all the properties of silk right now. I won't. I might need him to gag me again before I ruin this moment. Wait, shouldn't I *want* this moment ruined? This psycho who I'm sure has killed people is ripping my clothes off—metaphorically because remember silk is strong—and I'm worried about ruining the moment rambling about fabric.

"Take it off," he growls in my ear, his warm breath causing goosebumps to erupt all over me.

My hands shake as I push the gown down my body. Colin helps me step out of it. I'm still in a strapless bra and a thong, but I flush under his gaze anyway. I try to remind myself that he's seen me naked before so I shouldn't feel like this, but the way he looks at me is so intense. It's exactly like all the fantasies that ran on repeat for years, even before I met Colin.

I know it's not a fantasy or a game. I really do know this. But it's still all the things I want. A beautiful, powerful,

wealthy man, and kink. But weren't those fantasies about...
captivity and enslavement? Did I somehow invite this?

No. That's blaming the victim. And I don't blame the
victim, especially when the victim is me. But the thing is...
when he looks at me like this... making me feel all the things
I didn't know I could feel with a man... I don't feel like his
victim. I feel like I'm writing this story *with* him.

"Something blue?" he asks, arching a brow.

"I-I'm sorry, what?" I glance down and remember my bra
and panties are a pale blue. The garter that Will tossed at
the reception, matched.

I blush because suddenly I'm thinking about the fact
that Livia was at my wedding. She watched that horribly
awkward garter toss. She thinks I'm losing my virginity in
awful fumbling sex with Will right now.

"Take off the rest," he growls, not bothering to wait for a
response about the *something blue*. I'm pretty sure the question was rhetorical anyway. And I really really don't want to
say something stupid right now.

So I don't say anything, I just take off the bra and
panties. I'm not wearing anything like pantyhose. At this
point I think only old people wear pantyhose. And my shoes
actually didn't even make it up to the room. I've been so
nervous I forgot about that. They got left in the back of the
limo. My feet were hurting and so I slipped them off, and the
limo drove off with them.

First I was nervous about the fact that I married Will and
might be about to have awful sex—like for the rest of my
life. So I got halfway to the elevator before I even realized
my feet were bare. Then soon after that we were walking on
carpet. Then we got to the room, and I forgot again because
suddenly I was worried about... Colin.

"Get in bed," he says.

I do, and then he goes to the bathroom and turns on the

shower. He's in there a *long* time. Like way too long for a shower. I start to worry about what he's doing in there or if he had a freak accident. I'm about to get out of the bed to check, when the shower finally turns off.

A few minutes later he comes out wrapped in a towel. He turns the lights off and gets in bed with me.

"Go to sleep. We have to fly out early in the morning."

I should be more alarmed that he's taking me to an unknown destination on an airplane, but I can't get past the fact that it's my wedding night and I'm a virgin and he's telling me to go to sleep. I didn't imagine the way he looked at me, like I was something to be devoured. So why do I feel so... rejected and not up to his standards? And why do I want so badly to be up to his standards?

"But I thought you were going to..." I can't get the words out because... this man has basically kidnapped me. I mean yes I wanted him to come for me and stop me from having to spend my life with Will, but this is still illegal in about a thousand ways. I might have Stockholm Syndrome.

His hand snakes around my waist and he pulls me against his warm body. "Don't worry. I will deflower you, my little virgin. In Costa Rica."

Costa. Rica. There is this stupid part of me that wants to say: Why Costa Rica? What's in Costa Rica? But I know all about Costa Rica. Livia told me about Dayne's underground —secret, not literally under the ground—kink club. And I know that's where Colin is taking me. It's too big of a coincidence, and I don't believe in coincidences.

Colin strokes my hair. And I just can't help it. I say the stupid words out loud because maybe it is a coincidence and there's no connection whatsoever to where Livia went on her honeymoon. "Why Costa Rica?"

He chuckles. "Didn't Livia tell you about Costa Rica?"

We've hit that point where a word starts to sound like

nonsense because it's been said so many times. Costa Rica. Costa Rica. Costa Rica. It sounds like one word, like it could be someone's name. Meet my friend, Costarica. It also sounds like maybe it could be a spice. Like paprika. If I ever decide to to write a poem, I now know what rhymes with Costa Rica. Any gods in the universe? Please stop me now before I find a way to rhyme every spice in the average kitchen pantry.

"Didn't Livia tell you about the club?" he asks, when I don't reply. "I'm taking you to Costa Rica to train you. I told you... you're a sacrifice."

What the fuck does this mean? I tense, beginning to really worry he has intentions to kill me. Do people still do human sacrifice? Surely if that exists it's just tribes out in the middle of nowhere—like places where someone has to eat a virgin's heart every so often so the sun will keep rising.

I don't think Costa Rica is one of those places. I know the kink club isn't.

Then I remember he said most likely I would survive him. But this just worries me more. Is there a chance I won't survive him? And if so, why am I still not screaming and running from this man?

# 17

## MACY

I think I got maybe three hours of sleep. Despite everything that has led up to this moment, this morning has felt normal and domestic. Colin ordered us some breakfast. He didn't tie me up and feed it to me. We took showers—separately—and got ready, now we're on his private jet coasting down the runway. I'm strapped into my seat, and Colin is strapped into the seat across from me, doing some work on his laptop.

Jeffrey is in a seat across the aisle from us. I tried to cover my shock when I got on the plane and Jeffrey was here. Why is the butler coming with us on our honeymoon? All at once Colin's voice is in my mind telling me not to let that posh British accent fool me, and that Colin doesn't trust Jeffrey alone with me. At least not for long periods of time.

Why even have a butler if he can't trust him? And if he can't trust him in that way then why the hell is he coming with us to Costa Rica for a month? Will we be in Costa Rica for a month? I'm not sure about that part.

I know in the fake set-up I was supposed to be galli-vanting across Europe for a month, the cover story that lets

Colin do whatever the hell he wants to me for four weeks without a single soul missing me. I shudder at this thought, even as I feel the familiar throbbing ache between my legs. I know my reactions to this man are not normal.

What he's doing is not okay. This isn't the 1500s. You can't just force a woman to marry you and then train her to be your obedient sex toy. Though I'm not sure that happened in the 1500s. I think it was more forced breeding, and the man would find a separate whore back then. They were all about this idea of the chaste and innocent wife, which you know isn't true once the babies come out, but whatever. Those times were bad and weird.

And now I feel jealous. Is he going to have other women on the side? But even the pang of inappropriate jealousy can't suppress the obedient sex toy thing, and yeah, that thought is not helping. It only makes me more excited. I can feel the blush coming to my cheeks. I look down at my hands, willing this reaction to settle down. This is not normal. This is not normal. *This* is not normal.

I distract myself with thoughts of Colin's jet. Let's not downplay the jet. This is actually the most lush and biggest jet I've ever seen. Okay, so I've never really seen any private jets in person but... I've seen rich people movies. I mean, movies with rich people in them, not movies *for* rich people. I don't think there are special movies made just for rich people.

My mind goes down another one of those random bizarre dirty thought loops as I think about illicit super exclusive privately made porn for the wealthy. And now I'm wondering if custom made-to-order porn exists. What would it be like to have that job?

I close my eyes and take a deep breath while I try to shift my mind to my original distraction that was supposed to get me off the filthy train. Colin's jet is huge. I didn't even know they made jets this large for private use. I can't even imagine how much it costs to fuel it and keep it in the air. And the maintenance costs. Wow.

I find myself running imaginary calculations in my head for things I can't even begin to understand the cost of—like not even theoretically.

Before we got strapped in and started down the runway, I was given a tour. There's this sitting area, of course. It's right next to the cockpit at the front of the plane.

A large curtain separates us from another area. I thought maybe it was a bathroom or something, but no, it's a complete freaking living room. There's a super elegant white leather couch with an S-shaped design. It's one of those arty couches. Like what you find in a design or architecture magazine but don't imagine anybody actually owns or sits on. I swear rich people always seem to have expensive white couches... it's like... who cares if I spill wine on this fifty thousand dollar sofa, I'll just get another one!

There's a full bar in this area and the ability to cook light meals because doesn't everyone get the urge to cook at thirty thousand feet?

There's a giant flat screen TV opposite from the couch. Do we even really call them flat screens anymore? Or is this just the default TV now?

Then... another curtain. Surely the bathroom. Right? Nope. It's a bedroom with a king-sized bed and a closet much larger than one would expect to find on even the most luxurious of private planes. There's a door at the back of the bedroom right next to the bed and yes, that is the bathroom.

Finally.

It's huge. It's got a luxurious shower and all the amenities, and I can't quite understand how it's possible to have this stuff while flying through the air. I'm sure the technology behind this would fascinate me, and I plan to Google it if I'm ever allowed to be on the Internet again.

I'm not sure about that part, because even though I did want him to rescue me from a loveless marriage to Will, I was forced to sign myself over to him, and he has no intention of ever releasing me.

I can't imagine he'd allow me such easy access to the outside world without supervision, and if he DID supervise me, that would just be awkward. I can't Google the tech behind private jet amenities right in front of him. That's private Googling time—on the same level as porn for me.

"Where does the pilot or co-pilot pee if they have to go during a flight?" I just blurt these words out. I have no filter sometimes. I really can't help being this way. And my nerves over this entire situation aren't helping anything. I'm surprised my mind is capable right now of forming semi-coherent thoughts between the oscillating fears that he'll get tired of me and kill me, and the anticipation of what he's going to do to me sexually. And that's swiftly overridden by the guilt and shame for feeling anticipation over that rather than fear or revulsion, which I'm sure is what would be in the official "Acceptable human emotions for various scenarios" handbook, if such a book existed.

"What?" Colin asks, momentarily stunned by my weirdness. I think this is the first time he's looked up from his laptop since the plane got in the air.

I feel suddenly very self-conscious, but I plow on anyway. "Well, I mean... the bathroom is at the very back of the plane, behind the bedroom. You literally have to go past the bed. So... what if you're sleeping or having sex and the pilot or co-pilot has to pee? What then?" I wonder if they pee into a bottle or something at the front of the plane.

Colin chuckles and I'm sure I go bright red. I feel the heat in my cheeks, and do I want to call his attention to the bedroom right now? I was surprised and maybe just a little bit offended that my sex fiend captor hasn't already thrown me down on the bed, since there is one on the plane. I mean didn't he already make it clear that I basically exist now to serve his every whim and perversion?

"There's a second smaller bathroom, like what normal planes have, in the living area just behind the bar," he says.

"Oh." I vaguely recall seeing a few doors in the big living space that looked like they were possibly storage for food and bar stuff. Like a pantry or cabinets or something.

"Go explore the jet on your own if you like," he says, waving a hand in that direction as though there's some grand benevolence in this gesture. There has been no title on my part this morning, and I'm surprised he hasn't yet demanded it. Though for all I know, what he's typing on the laptop is a list of punishments for all my minor infractions.

I glance over to find Jeffrey clearly amused with me and my question. There's something else in his eyes I'm not sure I like. And I'm also not sure I don't like it, and that's more confusing and upsetting than the first thought. So I roll with the first thought. It's one thing to be turned on by Colin, it's another thing to be ready to go for any semi decently attractive male who decides he wants to lay claim to me. Also he's the butler and older. He's hot, but still, that feels so... I don't even have words for how it feels.

I notice Colin and Jeffrey aren't wearing their seat belts, I still am, which shows how unfamiliar I am with flying. I mean obviously we can take our seat belts off. What else would be the point of the different rooms and amenities on the plane?

I unlock the buckle and get up to stretch my legs, making my way back to the deeper interior of the plane and getting some much needed breathing room from the men.

Just as Colin said, there's a little bathroom behind the bar area much like what I'm used to from normal planes.

I make my way to the back of the jet to get a better look at the bedroom and especially the bathroom setup. The bed has a thick, downy white duvet on the top. I pull it back curiously and run my hand over the cool silver-grey silk sheets. I sigh and suddenly want a nap even though I haven't been awake long enough for a nap. I don't know how long one needs to be awake before a nap is appropriate but I feel like there's a protocol. Also, I am not a girl who naps. I'm a girl who works in the real world. Naps are for rich people.

I blush, as I realize that technically I'm now a rich person. I mean, I read that pre-nup. I get an allowance. And if he ever lets me go I get a very generous... severance package? That somehow feels like the right term because I'm here to fulfill a role. This isn't about hearts and flowers and kittens and long walks on a moonlit beach. Either way, I live with him in all this luxury now. I wonder if he'll even let me work at the library anymore.

I mean maybe I wouldn't need to do it full time, but I actually like my job. I like the people. I find the research interesting. And there are at least six professors who consider me completely invaluable and swear they'd be lost without me because nobody else at the library knows how to find a damn thing. I know we have the Internet now, and you'd think that would be enough. But there are many old and obscure texts that aren't online yet. And even those that are, are behind expensive paywalls, which the library has membership to but not every professor can afford on their own often meager salary.

I make my way through the door to the bathroom at the back. It's massive, so much bigger than you'd expect on a private jet. Marble floors and counters. Fixtures that I'm sure cost more than my apartment rent. The towels. Oh my god the towels. Thick, and plush, and so soft. I didn't even know fabric this soft existed. And he's got those tiny hand soaps.

Obviously he has a person who handles this sort of thing. There's no way a man—let along a man like Colin Black—would ever think about or desire to have fancy little soaps. They smell like lavender and peppermint, and I can tell they were made with essential oils. The smell is authentic, not artificial. And I imagine these were hand milled in some artisan boutique in France somewhere.

I'm not saying that's how they came to be... we're just in Macy's Brain now, and I attach a story to everything. I wonder if other people's internal monologues are like this. I blame all the time I spend alone. It's like when fairy tale heroines make friends with all the birds and squirrels... or household mice. It's an occupational hazard of introversion.

I gawk for a few minutes at the shower and the whirlpool tub—two things I still can't believe I'm finding on a plane—before making my way back to the living area.

I poke around in the bar for a bit and find a small refrigerator with some sandwiches. I barely ate anything at breakfast. A nice spread from room service was delivered to the Honeymoon suite which I picked over like one of those tiny bird women out on a date who pretend they don't eat food. But I wasn't trying to impress my new husband with the idea that I subsist entirely on oxygen. I was just too nervous. Will Colin be mad if I start eating his sandwich stash?

I don't know, but I'm suddenly ravenous.

These are really nicely made sandwiches—not like what some kid carries to school in their lunchbox. Thinly sliced rotisserie chicken with tomatoes and high quality cheeses. I can smell the vinegar. I love sub sandwiches with vinegar. There's fresh romaine and pickles on it. To be honest I've never had fresh romaine lettuce on a sub sandwich. It's normally that pre-shredded iceberg lettuce, the kind with zero nutritional content. It's basically like eating shredder paper. No taste, no vitamins, just filler.

The sandwiches are wrapped in the paper like you get at a sub shop. But this paper has no brand label on it, just an embossed gold foil seal, so I bet Jeffrey or an outside personal chef made them before the flight. Either that or it's such a high-end sandwich boutique that they consider visible branding gauche.

During my long time away from Colin while I was wedding planning, I found myself looking at a lot of fashion magazines and browsing all the clothes I would wear if I were Mrs. Black. And it became somehow very important to me in this imaginary world that I wouldn't wear visible designer labels. Because that screams middle class pretending to be rich. I mean I am middle class pretending to be rich, but there's no reason for the whole world to know it.

I find some ginger ale in the fridge and sit at the bar, swiveling the stool so I can view the television. It's set up for in-flight movies.

I jump when the curtain is ripped back and Colin walks in.

He arches a brow and strides into the room, pulling the curtain closed behind him. He wears a suit so well-tailored it's clearly bespoke, and shoes that must be the same—too completely unique to be a common designer, even a high end luxury designer. And of course in the short time of our acquaintance I've never seen an obvious label on anything. The most obvious label was the snowcap star on the top of his Montblanc pen.

Colin is the kind of man who has nearly everything custom-tailored to him and his exacting desires and demands.

His tie is very pale gray, only a single shade darker than

the crisp white linen of his shirt. My gaze drifts to his hands. He's got the sexiest hands.

I have this thing about men's hands. Large. Veined. Strong. He's well-groomed, and I can tell someone somewhere attends to his hands and nails—not in some girly feminine way—but because that level of impeccable detail speaks of one thing: Power. Someone so competent and in command that no detail escapes his notice. Nothing about him is unkempt or disheveled. Ever, most likely.

Meanwhile I feel like a hot mess just standing nearby and looking directly at him. I drop my gaze to my sandwich. Technically *his* sandwich.

"You know, there was a time when hands were chopped off for stealing food. But I'll need your hands later, so I'll let you keep them for now."

He says this so calmly I'm not even sure if he's kidding or not. I mean obviously yes, this is a historical fact about the penalty in some places for theft, but I doubt he'd chop off my hands. As he said, he'll need them, and I can only imagine the purposes he might need them for.

"I was hungry," I say around a giant mouthful of food. I almost choke when the vinegar in the sandwich hits the back of my throat wrong. It's like I'm a novice eater who hasn't yet figured out... swallow your food, then talk. I file this dining tip away for later.

He moves closer into my space, now a mere few feet away, glaring down at me as I pop the last bite of sandwich into my mouth and take a sip of ginger ale, once again with my mouth full. This man is never going to be able to take me anywhere upscale without me embarrassing him. I'm sure of it.

"You've gotten a little too casual with me," he observes.

I flush under his gaze, swallow the last of the sandwich, and inelegantly wipe my mouth with the back of my hand, paranoid I've got crumbs on my face. I wonder if, now that he's seen my truck driver table manners if he still finds me an appropriate wife to make him look good to the board.

Surely I'm not the kind of woman he should be parading on his arm for fundraising galas. I can't even remember how to properly hold a champagne flute. I know I'm supposed to hold it by the stem but I can't actually remember to do it on the rare occasions I have champagne.

I push my glasses up. It's this nervous tic adjustment I sometimes do. I usually don't even notice I'm doing it, but I'm so tense right now that I'm noticing everything: my breathing going in and out, the way the ambient air temperature in the plane's cabin feels against my skin, every fidget I make under the hard penetrating gaze of Colin Black.

Yesterday was so weird without my glasses. I swear, I tried to push them up a hundred times only to find they weren't there. Of course I'd packed them into my bags that had been delivered for me to the honeymoon suite.

"Macy, you try my patience. You know what I want from you."

I do know what he wants. The formality. The title. This piece of my surrender and obedience wrapped up like a tiny gift in shiny paper.

"I'm sorry, Master." I say it quietly. Jeffrey is just on the other side of this curtain, after all.

Colin winds a strand of my curly auburn hair around his fingers. For a moment I think he'll tug me down to my knees right here, the thought sending a sharp wave of arousal straight to my core. But instead he lets his hand drop and picks up the remote before going to the couch. He takes up so much space, sitting in the middle, his legs splayed out wide, his hands resting on the back. He looks like he's posing for a magazine cover... the picture of the illicit wealthy playboy.

He pushes a few buttons on the remote and soon my movie selection is a distant memory, replaced by panting, moaning, and begging, interspersed every few moments with threats and a cracking whip. The harsh crack against flesh is answered by sobs of "Please, Master, please, I'll be a good girl." I don't have to look to know he's got kinky porn playing.

"Take your clothes off, Macy. Let me see what now belongs to me."

My breath hitches in my throat. I know he's seen it all before, as recently as last night even, but the room was semi-darkened, and it was night. The last time before that was months ago. Also, he didn't have porn in the background at the time. I worry he's got the porn on to compare me to the girl on the screen, and it makes me so self-conscious.

"Turn away from me, watch the screen, and remove your clothes," Colin says. His voice has gone dark and guttural. I won't even be able to watch him to see if he's looking at me or the actress on the screen. Is this better or worse? To not know? I don't know why I should care. This isn't a real relationship. We aren't a couple. I'm just his... sacrifice... Even so, I'm so wet right now.

There is something severely wrong with the way my brain is wired. On the one hand, it's so awkwardly nerdy and full of trivial facts about nonsense nobody really cares about, and on the other hand, it's so darkly sexually twisted.

"Now, Macy. Or I'll call Jeffrey in here to watch you get your ass spanked."

"Yes, Master." I whisper the words but his answering, "Good girl," tells me he heard them just fine, even over the mewling whimpers of the girl on the screen.

I remove my top and jeans. I don't know if this is supposed to be a strip tease. I've never done that before. I wouldn't know where to start. The dominant on the screen lubes a toy and presses it into the girl's ass as she squirms and thanks him, arching back, trying to force the toy in deeper and faster. It's hard to know which of them is the more aggressive, the physically powerful male, or the tied-up woman.

My clothes are on the floor now, and I stand, the arousal flooding me as I watch the people on the screen, transfixed.

I hear the curtain open then and a posh British accent. "Finally unwrapping her?" Jeffrey says. "May I?"

"Help yourself."

I stand perfectly still while the sex sounds play in the background, and the crisp scent of the butler moves closer to me.

You don't think of butlers as sexy guys. I really only think about Batman's butler but that's probably a Macy quirk. Jeffrey is more like an older Batman than an Alfred. Except, you know, the accent.

I hold my breath as he prowls closer to me, assessing me more intensely than I've ever been assessed. It's just now I notice a whiskey glass in his hand. Brandy? Bourbon? Scotch? I don't know a lot about alcohol. But it's a strong-scented amber liquid he swirls around the glass. He takes a sip, his eyes never leaving me. There's stubble growing on his face. I've never seen him anything but perfectly clean-shaven.

This seems extremely odd to me. I mean from the start I thought maybe Jeffrey was some sort of bodyguard/butler combo but this seems outside of any parameters of employment—drinking on the job, I mean. My brain can't even process the rest. Is he on the job right now? Maybe he's using vacation time. Would he go with his employer on vacation? Maybe they're also friends. Though Colin doesn't seem like the kind of guy who has a lot of friends. This whole thing is so weird.

As if reading my mind, Jeffrey says, "Mr. Black, has a very generous employee benefits package. I get certain, *perks*, unavailable to other members of staff."

The *perks* part of that statement has goosebumps popping out over my skin.

He's done a full walk around me as he's talked, but now he's standing in front of me again, giving me a slow once-over. He ignores the porn that still rages on in the background, the intensity of the anal play ramping up.

I take in a sharp breath as his warm hand reaches out to cup first one breast, and then the other, as if testing their weight. It's like I'm some piece of livestock he's deciding whether or not he wants to purchase. I should be offended, but I'm too turned on for that.

"Will you be sharing her? Fully?" Jeffrey asks.

"Once she's been bred," comes the answer from the couch.

I can't believe those words just came out of Colin's mouth. And yet at the same time I can. I knew *heirs* were part of the contract I signed. It wasn't as though I had much choice in signing it, but I was going to be Colin's with or without the contract, not only because he'd clearly decided to keep me, but because I can't tamp down my foolish desire for him. The only thing signing the contract did was protect me. It left a legal paper trail. It would be hard for me to disappear now and for Colin to claim he'd never met me. At least I think that's true.

Also, being his *Mrs. Black* for the board members means people will see me. In public. He's not going to be able to keep me locked away in a basement somewhere, or keep me as some *Jane Eyre* style attic wife. I hope.

And anyway, he already let me roam on a long electronic leash for six months. So if I'm honest, I'm not even afraid he'll abuse me in any standard way. After all, he isn't going to want a *Mrs. Black* that looks like a hostage. He has a plan and an image to maintain. So I do have some amount of power in this arrangement, even though his mere presence often makes me forget this fact.

I jolt, surprised to feel Jeffrey's hand move between my legs. He holds me in place with one hand on my ass as the other explores my body.

"She's so wet," he murmurs, and I'm sure I blush hotter than I've ever blushed before. Damn my red hair.

"Is she?" Colin asks. I hear the thread of amusement in his voice. "Mrs. Black, is this true? Are you wet for him?"

"Y-Yes, Master."

I've realized since the contract signing why he wasn't bothered that I wasn't going to legally take his name. He doesn't care. Given our private contract, I don't have the automatic legal right to take his last name anyway—a realization which feels very odd to me. But Colin doesn't care what my name says on any piece of paper. He intends to refer to me as Mrs. Black. He intends to introduce me as Mrs. Black, and he intends for other people to think of me as and call me Mrs. Black. So my little rebellion of *not changing my name* means nothing.

Like anyone running in his social circle is going to ask to see my driver's license.

He will call me whatever he will call me. And the more I hear it, the more I like it, because it's him claiming me and showcasing that claim. It's him enfolding me into his family —not just some side piece or whore or toy or pet. Not even just his property or slave, but his wife. Mrs. Black. I'm not easily disposable. If we split it will be in the financial pages of the papers. It will be a scandal. It will hurt his stock prices. Maybe. Depending on what kind of business he runs. When there are heirs it'll be even messier. No, he needs to keep me, and he needs to keep me reasonably happy if he doesn't want questions. How would it look to the shareholders, after all, if Mrs. Black appeared to the world abused and mistreated?

"Mrs. Black," Colin says, jarring me out of my mental rambling. Jeffrey helpfully turns me to face my new husband. The way Colin looks at me is even more intense than Jeffrey's assessment. But his eyes never leave me. He never strays even for a second to the screen behind us where the moaning has gotten louder.

Colin crooks a finger at me. He points at the floor, and like some well-trained dog I drop to my knees before him. He strokes my hair and the side of my face.

"Good girl. Spread your legs."

I do, and that's when I feel Jeffrey's suit against me as he sits with his chest against my back. His hands move around to stroke my breasts and between my legs as Colin unzips his pants and frees his cock.

He doesn't say a word. He doesn't make any demands or orders. He doesn't instruct me. When really, maybe he should. I don't have the slightest clue what I'm doing here, but I lean closer. Tentatively I run my fingertips over him and then my hand. He's uncut.

I'm strangely excited by this. I've only really seen dicks on film and in images, and yet, a dick in it's natural state is somehow exciting. So many in porn are cut that it's kind of like finding a unicorn in the wild, this totally new and unexpectedly magical thing.

"Just how innocent are you, Macy?"

There's no judgment in his tone, just curiosity.

I look up at him and shrug, the shyness overtaking me again.

His hand continues to stroke through my hair. "I don't care what any stupid boy has told you. There's no wrong way to do this."

The way he's being with me right now is completely unexpected though I'm not sure what I expected. My only experience with him was a punishment and him going down on me. I guess I just assumed this experience would be like what I'd seen in porn, that he'd push me down and shove his cock down my throat and just not care how I felt about it.

A part of me finds that idea exciting, but I know the reality wouldn't evoke the same feelings. I grip his cock and slide his foreskin up over the tip and back down again. Then I experimentally lick, and taste him. He shudders when the wet tip of my tongue begins to explore him, and this alone gives me confidence to continue.

## 18

# COLIN

This girl is going to kill me. I never thought I was into the innocent ones—the ones who don't know what the hell they're doing, who need to be told every little thing. I do enjoy giving orders, but there was a certain kind of woman I thought I was into. And I find now that Macy's here, I was a complete idiot.

The reason none of the other women did it for me for very long was because they were being paid to be there. They'd been trained in the porn school of sex, which, as it turns out, isn't very accurate. Not because sex isn't as good in real life as it is in porn, but because artificial sex isn't any good, period—sex that's scripted and acted and performative.

Something can look good without feeling good, and something can look ridiculous and feel amazing. This is never more true than when it comes to sex. I don't think I realized just how tired I'd grown of all the performance and artificial fakery until this moment. The overly collagen-injected lips that made them too puffy and pouty to be real. The fake tits. The fillers and Botox. The overly made up faces. The overly sexy outfits. The choreographed and calcu-lated movements. The cat-like walking or crawling across the floor. The demure glances that were never really honest. The way they'd look up at me from the ground as they sucked my cock as though they didn't know if they were doing it right when we both knew they did, that they'd done it thousands of times. All part of the act. All part of the show I was paying for.

Even though ultimately they weren't that amazing. What they thought they knew, they didn't know at all.

Deep throating really doesn't do much for me. I guess for the men who like it, it's a power thing—this idea that some woman is willing to choke herself on your cock, that she's willing to give up oxygen just to pleasure you. But really, my cock ramming down the back of a woman's throat just physically does nothing much for me. Nerve endings aren't being hit in any special way after all. It only takes a moment of thought for anyone to realize this. But few take that moment.

A talented tongue though? Kissing, sucking the tip, swirling her tongue around, worshiping me, the vibration of her moan against my dick...now that? That is magic, and it's what Macy in all her innocence is actually doing right now.

She has no idea what she's doing, that much I know. But... the effect is still the best blow job I've ever received because it's not performance art. It's real. Just like Macy and this entire fucked-up situation.

She's not competing with other women who were well-trained to give me the sexual experiences they *thought* I wanted. A lot of men complain about innocence because it's inexperienced, but it's also without bad training, hang-ups, bad experiences. It's without artifice. It's without assump-tion. It's teachable and willing to learn.

If Macy is as innocent as I think she is, no man has been

a fucking tool and choked her with his dick because he saw it on porn once. And I'm eternally grateful for this. I may like to share my toys but my dick is the only one that goes in her mouth, ever. I never want her to have that experience with oral. I want it to always be like this—almost painfully sweet and genuinely eager. Not fake eager. I want her to like doing it.

She hesitates.

"Good girl," I murmur, as I stroke her hair, encouraging her. "Keep doing exactly what you're doing."

I take her hand and guide her to wrap it around my cock and show her what I want. With the combination of her pumping me with her hand, and her sweet mouth licking and sucking and kissing, her tongue dancing around the head of my cock, it doesn't take long for me to come.

When I do, I do the first thing I've done in this exchange that could be considered in any way aggressive, the one movement that reminds her she's not with a dog that's been housebroken. I wrap my hand possessively around the back of her neck and hold her in place as I come down her throat.

"Swallow." I say the word quietly, but I know she heard me. Jeffrey continues to pet her like the good girl she is as her throat works to swallow every last drop of the mess she created with her sweet mouth.

I pull out of her and zip up. "Good girl." I lean back and watch Jeffrey. He's teased her this entire time, his hands moving from her perfect tits to her dripping cunt. His hand drifts between her legs again, and this time he's done teasing.

I'm not sure what it says about me, but I love watching another man touch what's mine. Maybe that's not normal, but fuck what's normal. There's something so primal about the whole thing, that I will pass her around and watch her come and lose herself to any man I point to, and that she'll love every second of it. That she'll give herself to me in such a complete way, that she will surrender this fully. That her lines are my lines, and I have almost no lines.

What can I say? I like to watch. And the *American Psycho staring at yourself in the mirror while fucking* thing just doesn't do it for me.

Macy looks at the ground, distracting herself staring at my shoes.

"Mrs. Black. Look at me. I want you to look at me while you come for Jeffrey. You were such a good girl; it's time for your treat."

Her large pale green eyes rise to mine. Those glasses, man. I can't get over them. This is the first women with glasses I've ever fucked—such a strange thing to realize. I think there was a librarian role play once, but this girl is an *actual* librarian. A virgin librarian with nerd glasses. Could I be any more of a cliché right now?

"Jeffrey!" I bark, realizing what he's about to do.

"Yes, Sir?"

He's still so formal, even now. "Don't penetrate her. That's for me."

"Oh, right."

He sounds ridiculously proper when he says those words, so proper in fact I'm sure he'll finish it off with a *Cheerio* and then just exit the plane in midair to go on a fox hunt.

He forgot Macy was a virgin. I doubt he could accidentally pop her cherry with his fingers, but still, that territory is mine to explore the first time. He'll get his turn later.

Macy's eyes start to stray again, so I place my hand under her chin and raise it so her gaze is forced to mine.

"If you don't hold my gaze, there will be punishment. Do you understand?"

"Y-yes, Master."

I nod, pleased that she's not pretending not to know what I want. Macy's too smart for that shit. She probably thinks she has a punishment coming for eating the sandwich but those sandwiches were prepared for both of us, and I'm not such a control freak that she has to ask me every time she needs to pee or eat. I'd find that level of micro-management completely exhausting. And I don't need it to own every corner of her soul. By the time we get done in Costa Rica, she's going to know exactly what the word Master means.

She finally let's herself go, jerking against Jeffrey's hand, unable to hold back the sweet whimpers as my thumb caresses her jawline.

"Yes, just like that... give us your pleasure."

She shudders a final time and her eyes drift closed. Jeffrey presses his finger to her mouth, the finger she made wet. Without instruction or struggle, she opens and allows that finger to penetrate her mouth as she moans around it. I need to take this girl in a way I've never needed to take anyone. This unsettles me more than I'd like.

"Leave us," I say to Jeffrey, and like the good little house servant he ultimately is, he quietly gets up and leaves. I pick her up and carry her to the bedroom, tucking her in to the silk bedding.

"Get some rest."

She opens her eyes. "Aren't you going to stay?"

I shake my head. "No, from this point on there are things you have to earn, and sharing my bed, is one of them."

# 19

## MACY

I don't wake until the plane lands. And even then, I don't wake until I'm being literally carried off it. I don't have to open my eyes to know it's Colin carrying me, and I'm glad it isn't a paid member of his staff. I can sense him in this almost supernatural way. There's a way he moves and a solidity to him that other people don't have.

Underneath all of that is his scent, a combination of the barest hint of cologne, and him. There are women who spend a long time putting on makeup in such a way to make it seem as though they aren't wearing any at all, like they're just naturally that beautiful. That's the illusion. And most men who say they don't like makeup on a woman, that's what they mean. They love makeup, but they love makeup where the illusion is so painstaking and complete that they can't tell it's there. They can't smell it. They can't see it. They can't taste it.

It's completely silent and invisible like servants under the stairs.

This is the way Colin wears cologne. It's so barely there,

that for a moment I might be able to fool myself that he just naturally smells this way.

I'm still naked, but at least he's wrapped me in the sheet from the bed. It feels decadent being carried from the jet wrapped in silk. He deposits me into the back seat of whatever luxury car will be driving us to our location and gets in the other side with me. Despite all the random fun facts I know about absolutely everything, luxury cars is not on that list. I couldn't tell you the difference in a Bentley, a Bugatti, and a Lamborghini. Though at least I know those words, so that's something, I guess.

When the car starts to move, Colin speaks. "I know you're awake. I felt your breathing change."

I think he means he noticed that big obvious sniff I took of him like I was a dog engaged in social bonding when he was carrying me a few minutes ago.

"Why didn't you wake me to get dressed?" I ask.

"Because I don't want you dressed right now, Mrs. Black. If I want you naked, you'll be naked. Be grateful for the sheet."

This is the point at which a normal woman would start yelling or cursing or throwing things or at least be internally offended. Or maybe even cry, scream, or beg. There's a huge range of the emotional experience I could be having and expressing right now—if I had more sense.

Given some of my circumstances, I could almost be forgiven if I were too afraid to fight back. But this isn't a fear thing, it's a... I desperately want to ride his cock, thing.

I don't want to fight him, not because I'm truly afraid he'd harm me, but because he might let it slide and do nothing. There's something between us that I don't want to break. I don't care how archaic it sounds or how wrong it is, but I like his control. I like the ruthless power that rolls off him. I've always been this way.

I was barely able to be in Soren's presence without spontaneously kneeling. Being in his energy made me want to be owned and dominated in ways which aren't polite to admit to and which definitely are not feminist.

Then there are the general twisted fantasies which I've had way longer than feels normal or appropriate to me. I don't know exactly why I'm like this or if there's something wrong with me. But I know I respond to Colin's power, and after the blow job on the plane, there's a part of me that—sick and wrong or not—trusts him to keep me safe.

He didn't hurt me, or push me, or force anything on me. He was gentle and let me handle it my way. And it made me want to. Though I won't lie and pretend I haven't had rough fantasies. This is the big fight within me, the reality that being a real captive isn't a fantasy, and yet... here's Colin the kidnapper who feeds me brunch on the fancy plates.

With every piece of this situation that locks into place, I am more ensnared, but feel somehow more safe which I know is crazy because Colin is dangerous. This isn't a role he's playing. I don't know why I'm so sure about this, but I really think he's killed people. I feel unhinged thinking that, like maybe it's just my wild imagination, but there's this dark coiled thing inside him that I'm just happy isn't aimed in my direction. I still worry maybe someday it could be.

As if sensing my thoughts, Colin pulls me against his chest, his fingers stroking through my hair.

"Master? Where are you taking me?"

"To the dungeon," he says. And I'm not sure if he's kidding or not. But he doesn't say anything else so I don't ask any more questions.

About half an hour later, we end up at a huge isolated resort. Small gold lettering inset into the brick beside an iron gate reads: "The Dungeon."

As soon as he mentioned Costa Rica, I knew we'd be

coming to Dayne's club. I just didn't realize it was actually called *The Dungeon*. I'm pretty sure Livia doesn't know either. After all, there isn't some giant tacky glowing neon sign announcing this name. And as Colin gives his access code and we pull through the large iron gate and around to the main building, there's no obvious sign. Nothing on the grounds, nothing on the door.

The only indication this place even has a name was that small, tasteful gold engraving on the brick outside the gate which I'm sure nobody really ever reads, except me, but I google literally everything, so I'm probably a statistical anomaly.

Colin leaves me in the car to go inside. He's in there for a few minutes, and I'm glad the window is up between me and the driver. I'm feeling more naked now and being completely covered by a giant piece of silk for some reason isn't helping much.

It's funny how our brains work that way. I'm more covered up right now than most of the clothes I wear, but a sheet isn't clothing. And my knowledge of that makes me somehow still naked, even fully covered. I'm still pondering this when Colin returns to the car and the driver takes us down several winding paths away from the main building to a very large house with it's own iron gate. The engraving outside of this one is "The Cottage". I would never put the person who named these buildings in charge of nail polish naming. Could you imagine? Instead of colors like "Salacious Gossip" we'd have "Red" and "Pink". Half the reason I choose any nail polish color is the name.

There's a live guard here. The driver stops to speak to him, then the gate opens and we pull in.

"This is Dayne's cottage. Soren arranged for us to use it during our stay," Colin says.

*Cottage* is the most wrong description I can think of for

this place. It's really more like a mini-mansion. There's a pool and a hot tub, and three ridiculously large bedrooms— like individual loft apartments, all with their own bathrooms. There's a full kitchen and dining room and living room and game room. These are just the parts I see as Colin leads me to one of the bedrooms on the second floor.

"This will be your room," he says taking me inside one of apartment-sized rooms. And I'm being literal here, this room is actually bigger than my apartment. I could probably fit my apartment inside this room twice and still have a little space left over for a medium-sized dog.

"I get my own room?" Suddenly I'm wondering if we're going to be one of those married couples with separate bedrooms who never have sex. Or maybe couples with separate bedrooms have *more* sex? There's a theoretical way in which that works. If you can have it all the time, any time, just inches away from you, do you really want it anymore? Isn't that why most marriages grow stale and the sex goes away? Or is it because of kids banging on the door and puking in the middle of the night? I'm not sure. Maybe it's a bit of both.

Now part of me worries Colin has some virgin fetish to the point that he plans keep me a virgin forever while maybe enjoying my mouth. God what the fuck is wrong with me? This thought really turns me on. I mean I don't want to be an eternal virgin or anything, that's kind of depressing. But the *idea* of this gets me going. The fantasy.

And then I remember the *heirs* part of the contract I signed. Of course I'm not going to be a virgin forever. Unless he just turkey bastes me into pregnancy. Then he could have the best of all worlds, I guess.

I stand in the hallway outside the room just zoning out thinking about this as Jeffrey brings my bags in and deposits them on my bed. I guess he's back to being the butler again and we're going to pretend that sort-of devil's threeway on the plane didn't happen.

"Get dressed," Colin says.

"For what? Where are we going?" I stand in the hallway, still wrapped in the sheet from the plane. By now a part of me wants to just cut this fabric up and sew it into an evening gown, we've gotten to that level of coziness—me and the sheet.

"It's our honeymoon, Macy. We're going to the Sloth Sanctuary." He says this as though this should be the most obvious thing in the world, as though it's impossible to come to Costa Rica on your honeymoon and not visit the sloths. It's just not done, apparently.

I nod and go back to my room to pick out an appropriate outfit for a day of honeymoon tourist attractions. But inside I'm giddy.

Livia told me all about the Sloth Sanctuary in Costa Rica, and I was so jealous. First she had these three hot men, her own man harem, all engaging in her dark dirty fantasies —and let's be honest, *my* dark dirty fantasies, and they took her on an amazing honeymoon where she got a private tour of sloths. And I wanted a private tour of sloths, too. It's not that I need to copy everything Livia does, like some robot person without their own independent personality, but there's a reason we're friends. We like a lot of the same stuff.

Though, really, who doesn't like sloths?

We don't bother to eat, I mean I had that giant sandwich on the plane. I'm still good, and Colin probably ate while I was having my post-orgasmic nap.

I've kind of been shoving a lot of that to the back of my mind. The butler gave me an orgasm while Colin smugly watched on. How am I supposed to feel about that? I mean I know how I'm *supposed* to feel about it. I'm supposed to feel horrified, used, abused, dirty, ashamed. I'm supposed to be scared of what's coming next. But that's not what I really feel.

My experience with Colin that first day... with the punishment and then in his bedroom, and my experience with him last night where he didn't even do anything, and my experience with him on the plane... where he was so surprisingly gentle and encouraging... all these things add up to me feeling safe with him. I don't feel judged by him. I don't feel afraid of him even though I know I should. If there's any man a smart woman should feel afraid of, it's Colin Black. But the way he's been with me, the way I feel when I'm with him... it just doesn't add up to all the things I'm *supposed* to feel.

Instead, I want to pinch myself to see if I'm dreaming. My mind goes back to Colin's "Wish, granted", and I shiver. Be careful what you wish for?

Maybe I am a little afraid, afraid of getting everything I've ever wanted, and afraid maybe there's another shoe that will drop, or it'll become too much and I'll fall out of the fantasy before I've had the chance to completely surrender to it. But I can't help but be so grateful that I'm not in Europe right now with Will, having repulsive missionary sex with a man and a life I don't want.

Despite everything society and people I know might think about it, Colin might be the life I *do* want.

# 20

# COLIN

By the time we return from the sloth sanctuary, Macy is relaxed. She must have squealed in delight at the sloths twenty times or more while we were there. Normally, if a woman did that I'd be done with her. I'm not into these giggly silly girls, but it's different with Macy. I felt this odd warmth at her happiness. It was as if my Grinch heart grew two sizes today.

I arranged for the private behind-the-scenes tour, which isn't as easy to get as one might think—even with my money. Soren got me the details on it from when he was on his honeymoon with Macy's friend. I stood back and watched her cuddle and feed baby sloths most of the afternoon. I didn't participate. My inner sense of self is already taking a beating from my happiness over Macy's happiness, me holding a baby sloth and feeding it like a proud new father was out of the question.

This isn't how it was supposed to be. Soren was giving me a fucking virgin sacrifice that I could train and use according to all my twisted dark desires. I was going to breed an heir—probably several—and keep Macy as my pet, and her feelings weren't going to play into any of it. But I wasn't prepared for this girl.

I wasn't prepared for this bizarre mix of nerdiness and sexiness. I've never experienced a woman like this before. She may be innocent, but she's eager. She wants me. I told myself I didn't care if the woman Soren gave me wanted me or not. I didn't care because she was mine. Mere property. Payment for Soren's fuck-up.

I thought I wanted a woman who was afraid of me. Genuinely afraid. Not pretend afraid. I thought I wanted genuine begging. Genuine desperation. Because I'm fucked up. I've always been fucked up. In a different set of circumstances I would be the serial killer living with a lot of stuffed animals—taxidermy, not toys. But the only genuine thing I want from Macy is her surrender, and that doesn't have to be dramatic or traumatic.

The longer I'm around her, the more I want this to be mutual. I still want a toy, a pet, a plaything. And I fully intend to share her. But I don't want her to be a traumatized victim huddling in a basement with tears streaking down her face while she begs me not to hurt her. Even the idea causes a sick feeling to form in my stomach.

When you have my kind of money, it isn't logistically difficult to kidnap a woman, keep her under lock and key, and do whatever the hell you want with her, including sharing her with your equally rich and amoral friends. But my new desires—her happily going along with this, her desire for everything, including being liberally shared—require finesse.

I've long held this perfect image in my mind of mascara streaks on a woman's face, her wide scared eyes staring up at me, and the rush of power. I don't know what's wrong with me. I should probably be in prison... if not for my desires, at least for the people I've made disappear. Macy is lucky, I've at least never killed nor wanted to kill a woman. So she's always been safe on that score, no matter how hard I sold the bluff—even to myself. If she'd tried to remove that tracking bracelet or told anyone the truth I could have just moved up my timeline.

I thought I wanted something real and not a game. I thought I wanted a woman who belonged to me, one who wasn't acting. But I find I have no true taste for this woman's suffering. I need her in this with me, fully committed, and the only way to do that is to have her trust, her willing surrender to my twisted games.

Is that even possible? I've gotten a glimmer that despite her innocence she has at least a bit of a kink streak. The phone call with her friend months ago at breakfast, intrigued me forever. I at least knew from her masturbation schedule that Macy has a strong healthy interest in sex, which made it even more puzzling how such a beautiful woman could be nearly thirty and still untouched. And I knew from her response to me both that first too-brief morning, and this morning on the plane, that she's definitely more than meets the eye.

She didn't react in a prudish way to the porn on the screen. And she didn't pull away when Jeffrey started to touch her. I'd expected her to get shy or uncomfortable or upset or beg, and I wasn't sure what I'd do about it.

Macy and I sit together in the back of the car. We've just returned to The Cottage. There's a private, fully outfitted dungeon in the basement which she hasn't seen yet, but she's about to. I want to start her training before I unveil her to others. Screw Soren's rules. He'll get his virgin sacrifice, but she's mine, and I refuse to be managed by that asshole.

I don't know what to do with the feelings Macy creates inside me—the loss of control I feel around her. That tiny sense of fear that I've never experienced before... *What if something happens to her*? Before Macy I'd never thought that thought before in my life. The first night when she ran from me, it gripped me in a kind of terror I didn't know I could feel at all. About anything. I didn't think I was capable of feeling it. Every moment with this woman has been like this.

It wasn't rational. There was no reason for me to give any kind of shit if she died out in the cold woods. It was stupid for her to run. That's just natural selection at work. That's what I would have told myself with any other woman. But this girl was different.

And then everything after that... from her bizarre trust under my touch when no part of her should trust me, to her weird facts, to the way she came apart and surrendered under my tongue. I needed six months just to get my head sorted. I seriously considered not coming back for her.

I picked up the phone at least a dozen times to call Soren, call it off, and get him to find me someone else or extract the payment from him in a different way. Macy is too dangerous to my sanity. Let her wear that bracelet forever, I told myself. What do I care? Maybe she'll never take it off. Maybe one day she'll realize she can. Who the fuck cares? Let her stay in a cage of her own making until she decides to step out of it. What difference does it make to me? As long as I was free of the redheaded witch and her strange spell, I could go back to the way my life was before.

I could give up the desire and need for this thing to be real. Paying the whores was safer. It was cleaner. Ironic though that is.

I wonder what Will would have done if, after marrying her, he'd come up to the honeymoon suite to deliver her to me but I hadn't been there to collect. I was so close to letting that happen. Would he have consummated the marriage? Would he have kept the ruse going and tried to contact me? Would he have kept her for himself? In five years would these two be living lives of quiet desperation because I was too afraid to take what I wanted? I've never been afraid of anything. And now I feel like I'm afraid of everything, at least where Macy is concerned.

I realize now, while we're sitting in the car together, the driver pulling us through the gate, that I don't want her trust. I have it. Even if she doesn't know it, I have it. As stupid and wrong as it is, on some deeper level she senses I'm not going to harm her—at least on purpose. She new it well before I did. There are a million ways I could hurt her from fear and sheer stupidity but I try not to think about that.

No, I have her trust. Now I just need to not lose it. And the biggest question rattling through my brain is... how do I get all my needs and darkest desires met, and bring her along for the ride as my *willing* toy? How do I guide her and myself through this experience I think, inexplicably, we both want?

# 21

## MACY

Colin has been quiet the entire ride back to the cottage. I have no idea what he's thinking. He seems tense and on edge. This isn't the reaction you'd expect from someone who's just been to a sloth sanctuary. I felt self-conscious at first because he wasn't participating, but eventually I gave in to the overload of cuteness.

We had access to everything. And this wasn't the official behind-the-scenes tour. I know this because when Livia told me about everything, I scoured the internet to learn all about the sloth sanctuary's behind-the-scenes tours. They are a little exclusive, but they aren't *super crazy wealthy people* level exclusive. And what Livia described to me was above and beyond what the website offered.

No, this was... much more "I know a guy", than that. I'm pretty sure we got the same ultra-exclusive tour that Livia and her guys got. Colin and I were there for hours and were even served a meal in a private fancy dining room in a building hidden from view of the public. Colin just watched me during the meal. I won't lie, I felt a bit like a bug kept in a jar for observation.

Even so, there's something peaceful in his stoic demeanor. He's like a human version of the library, and I'm comfortable in libraries. My mind is so loud that I need the quiet.

He guides me into the house, his hand on my upper arm like he's guiding a captive to the dungeon. And then we go down a set of stairs and it actually *is* a dungeon.

I never thought you could call a dungeon "swanky" but, this is about the most luxurious and elegant room I've ever seen that's intended for tying people up and whipping them.

"Master?"

"I'm glad you haven't forgotten my name," he says as I take it all in.

"Only in private, though, right? In public I'm supposed to be your wife. What do I call you in public?"

"You *are* my wife." He sounds annoyed.

Colin does that one-handed tie-loosening thing that drives me crazy. I don't know what it is about the way a man jerks his tie loose like that that sends me into a frenzy, but it's not just me. It's pretty much a meme in romance novels so... I feel like I'm in good company with this. One of my few *weird things* that doesn't feel quite so lonely.

"It depends on what you mean by in public," he says, his eyes never leaving mine.

I lick my lips. I keep waiting for him to take off his shirt, or his jacket at least, but he remains dressed.

"I-I'm sorry Master, what?" Did he just say something?

He chuckles. "Distracted, Mrs. Black? I said there will be plenty of times in public when you'll call me master, but you'll know by the venue. It'll be obvious what those places are. In most public places, I don't care what you call me. Just play the role of the respectable wife. You can pick your own pet name."

I can't even imagine coming up with a normal couply pet

name for Colin. Just the idea of it almost makes me burst out in laughter. I wonder idly if I could get away with calling him my little marshmallow.

"A-and what will you call me... in public, I mean?"

"Depends on where we are... in some venues, whore, slut, pet. In normal places... I haven't decided..." he gives me a long slow once over, as though he's a computer running a program to determine an appropriate name.

My heart is fluttering so fast. If there are times in public I'll call him master and he'll call me... those other things... it means we're going to the resort's public dungeon... and maybe more places or situations like that. The things we do won't just be behind closed doors. Is he going to share me with more than just Jeffrey? A thrill slides through me which I know probably shouldn't be there.

This would all be different if I'd met him on a kinky dating app. It would be different if I'd agreed to be his sub, but that's not the case. Still, the way he's been with me isn't anything like what one would expect in a situation like this. Maybe my body isn't crazy for trusting him. The most harmful thing he did to me was let me go, to believe I'd have to spend my life with a man I didn't love.

But I don't love Colin either. I don't really know him. I'm attracted, sure, but however this goes, at least I didn't choose him. I'm just along for the ride.

But *could* I love him? I turn this thought over in my head. I don't want to love Colin. I can't think of anything more dangerous than falling for this man. I have to keep it about sex and remember that I didn't volunteer to be with him. I was coerced into signing that contract. I'm obligated to produce heirs!

If I think these thoughts enough, I might be able to actually remember them, instead of getting sucked into this kinky Barbie Dream House fantasy. No matter what happens, I can never, ever let myself fall in love with this man. Even as I think it, I know it's already a lost cause. I'm so screwed.

Women and men don't have sex the same. I know, I know, I'm still a virgin, but... I'm well read. The point is, we can pretend to be like a man. Drink like a man, do business like a man, fuck like a man. But we can't really do any of that. Most of us can't drink a man under the table because we have smaller bodies on average so most of us biologically can't handle the same amount of alcohol. Some women can do business like a man, so I'm not taking it back to the 1950's here or anything, but still, we have to be "go getters" and never relax, and for most it's unnatural and wears you down hormonally after a while. Again, go girl power and all that, these are just biological realities for most. Don't shoot the messenger. And then... there's sex, the biggest issue of all. And our prime enemy? Oxytocin, the cuddle hormone.

Women with a lot of experience can learn to just ignore this hormone, but it's a kind of hormonal bonding, like out of some werewolf book. And it's the primary reason why men can emotionally separate sex and love in ways that most women can't. And that's the danger here, that no matter what my mind wants or what's smart, the more he touches me and makes my body feel good, the more I'm going to bond to him and mistake that big stew of swirling hormones for love.

I've been casually glancing around the room while my mind went on this obsessive fact spewing holiday, but now when I look at Colin, he ensnares my gaze, and I can't bring myself to look away again.

"Undress, Macy. I'm ready to start teaching you how to be a good and obedient wife."

And... this pair of panties is ruined. Seriously what is wrong with me? These kinds of things shouldn't excite me.

On the up side, I've finally managed to completely ditch my inappropriate crush on Soren. Soren, who? A part of me thinks I just feel guilty for my kinks full out, because I always find some kind of shame or guilt to attach them to. With the way Soren made me feel, it was guilt that he was Livia's husband, even though we never did anything, and I would never betray her. So that was easy to justify. Of course I should feel a little guilty for that. I was lusting over her man—one of them anyway.

Now with Colin it's the way I came to be in his care. But is there any situation in which I wouldn't have these guilt and shame feelings? I feel wrong that I'm still technically a virgin—like there's something broken in me, or else surely I wouldn't still be... untouched. Though that's a stupid way to think of it, I have most definitely been touched.

I feel wrong for my desires—another thing that feels broken. I just feel perpetually... wrong. And I'm not sure what the solution to that is. All I know is that my mind is a constant hamster wheel of noise. Normal people might take up meditation, but am I crazy to think Colin can help me be quiet inside? That day he punished me wasn't at all what I expected. I can fantasize and touch myself and bring myself to orgasm, but you can't self-spank. I'd always fantasized about it, but in the end, it still felt nothing like what I thought it would feel like when it finally happened.

Part of me thought it would never happen. I couldn't imagine myself telling a guy I'd like him to tie me up and spank me. I already felt so out of step with the rest of the world and everybody in it that I didn't want to call attention to yet another thing.

But when Colin had me in his dungeon... when it was actually happening, it felt... peaceful and quiet. Like standing under a waterfall out in the forest. The warmth on my skin was like lying by the pool in the sunlight. I could be quiet inside my own mind, if only for a few moments, and more than the pleasure and fantasy, I want to keep having that. And I didn't feel judged by him. He'd initiated it, and it was out of my power and control, and so I didn't have to feel the awkwardness and shame I might have otherwise felt.

I mean yes, I know... it's not the fifties. I'm allowed to have desires. Kinks are okay. I know all this stuff intellectually, but you can't just change your wiring on command. Though maybe I could do it if Colin commanded it.

"Well?" Colin says. His arms are crossed over his chest as he watches me and waits for me to comply with his demands while I'm busy spacing out.

"A-aren't you going to undress?" I ask when he just stands there, watching and assessing like he does.

A slow head shake. "No. Like sharing my bed, that's another thing you'll have to earn."

I've seen him without a shirt one time, the night I ran away, but it seems that was just meant as a preview to torture me... *All this can be yours with absolute obedience...*

My hands shake as they move to unbutton my jeans. He's seen me naked multiple times. I repeat this mantra in my head over and over. Why should I feel nervous? And things were brightly lit on the plane. The lighting is dim down here. Why should I feel self conscious when he's already seen me naked so many times?

I'm going to give myself a panic attack. I take a deep breath and slowly start to peel the clothes from my body as Colin's hungry gaze takes in every movement.

"Get on your knees and spread your legs, like you did on the plane."

My breath flows slowly in and out of me as I follow his order and wait. The quiet is upon me now, inside the peace of his commands. All the inane mind chatter and random facts that otherwise swirl around my head fall away as I stare at his shoes and the part of his suit I can see from the ground. I'm barely aware of my fingers digging into the carpet.

I jump when his hand is suddenly in my hair, petting me.

"Good girl."

He begins to slowly circle me.

"M-Master... when are you going to..." I can't say the word deflower, it's too old-fashioned even for me. I mean I've thought the word, and sometimes it shows up in my morning *me time*, but I don't ever say the word *out loud*.

He chuckles as if he can read my mind, and I'm sure he probably can. My facial expressions practically have closed-captioning. "Deflower you?" he asks, just shamelessly putting that word out there.

Okay, I do like that word. I like all the dirty, politically incorrect, wrong things it implies.

I nod, blushing.

"At the ritual. I told you, you're the sacrifice." He says this as if it's an item on a to-do list he's mentioned to me a hundred times. There is no emotion or added significance. It's more like *I told you, I'll pick up the milk after I get off work.*

It's only now that I realize all of Soren and Colin's talk about me being a sacrifice wasn't some kind of metaphor or inside joke. It wasn't just that I was being given to Colin to pay some debt.

No, he's being somehow literal. There's a plan, and it's been in place since Soren gave me to him.

"When is this happening?" My voice comes out way calmer than I feel.

"Tomorrow night."

# 22

## COLIN

"You trust me, don't you?" I ask the question not expecting a reply, at least not expecting an *honest* reply. I've never done this particular dance with a woman because it's never been real, not even in the vanilla relationship version. But I've watched women deny men many times—not their bodies, but their truth.

In my world, few women deny the men in my social circles their bodies, but they all guard secrets. They won't confess their love unless they believe it will get them something of value like a ring or a house in the Hamptons. And they never confess their trust. Too many women have been burned by trusting men in my world.

It's too easy for a man with money and power to destroy any woman who trusts him. If she doesn't have her own empire he can destroy her financially simply by removing his presence from her life, especially if he was very smart about the pre-nup, or if he only kept her as a concubine on the side, constantly promising her more, but never delivering.

Getting used to a certain type of lifestyle is like a drug,

and he can pull it away at any moment. Once tasting the luxe life, most of these women aren't willing to give it up. They make endless concessions and guard their emotions. If Cinderella's story had continued, I sometimes wonder if the prince would have had another woman on the side while she pretended everything was perfect in her fairly tale just so she could stay in the castle a little while longer.

For many women, it's not a fairy tale. There's a dark side. He can cheat. He can trade her in on a newer, younger, fresher model when she becomes too *last season*. As a result, many women in my world simply do not trust. They put on the fake smile, they do the performance art blow jobs, they dress pretty like our little dolls and get all the Botox and injectibles and other treatments and surgeries, the butt lifts, the breast enhancements—all in the hopes of keeping our eyes from straying to the next pretty young thing constantly on the prowl for our attentions.

They don't make waves, hoping against hope that all this work they're putting in will at least buy them a little loyalty and security, even if he's flying to the south of France with his secretary on the side. At least she'll have the ring. The title of Mrs. And some of those last names are currency all on their own. There are names everyone knows and those names open doors.

She believes she can trade a bit of her soul. She may not really be *The One*, but she'll be the one on his arm at all the formal events, the one with the respect, the one all his friends know, even if she can't always be the woman who holds him spellbound in the bedroom. She won't be the one he loves above all things, including his own hedonistic pleasure and the newness of getting his dick wet in a new supermodel every weekend, but at least she won't be his dirty little secret.

It's only a bit different if the woman has money of her

own, an empire of her own. But even so, money can't solve a broken heart. To let a man in who can have anyone is dangerous ground to walk upon. And we know it... the men. We know it and we play upon that weakness. We play up our dominance and show that we know we have all the cards, but it's only because we could, theoretically, lose all of our power under the thrall of the right woman. We can never let them know how much power they could hold.

Each side must play their role. She must resist falling for the man who can't fall under her spell, and he must resist her spell.

Because of these all too harsh realities in my world, I expect a fight or denial from Macy when I ask if she trusts me.

"Yes, Master, I trust you."

I wonder if she's the most foolish woman in the world. Definitely she's the most naive. Yes, I realize I kidnapped her, forced her to sign documents legally binding herself to me... promising me heirs for fuck's sake, but... to just gift wrap her trust and lay it at my feet like this? To not even pretend to deny or refuse me her honesty? To not hold even the tiniest thing back from me?

If this were anyone but Macy, this sweet and naive admission would be her downfall. Macy will still fall, but she'll fall *with me*, not beneath me. I won't abandon her when she hits the ground. She holds an ace she doesn't even know she has. I've had plenty of women—an endless fucking parade of them. All flavors. Exotic types. Worldly women. Women most men couldn't dream of having on their arm even for a night. And yet... every single one of them left me cold.

Except Macy. I can only assume that whatever thing inside me is dead, somehow is allowed to breathe when she's near. And that to me, is worth everything. Even the potential loss of power.

"You feel safe when my hands are on you," I say, as though I need to clarify this. There's something pathological inside me that needs to know exactly what she means when she confesses trust in a man little better than a rabid dog. She's not a stupid woman. At least she's not book stupid. Maybe she's street stupid, but she doesn't strike me as that either. Her response to me seems to have nothing to do with what her mind tells her. No, she's following a different lure altogether, a different way of knowing and sensing that I can't begin to guess the finer points of.

"Yes, Master." Her voice catches when she says it, and I stroke my fingers across her downturned face, to feel the tear that escapes.

"Do you know how foolish it is to trust me or feel safe in my presence?"

Her shoulders are shaking now. This wasn't what I was planning to do with her down here. And yet, here we are.

"Y-yes, Master."

I swallow past the lump in my throat and say something I've known to be true since the moment I first saw her. "It's foolish, but in your case, it's true. You are safe with me. But this doesn't mean I won't push you or ask things of you which may seem... unconventional."

This is quite possibly the mildest way to describe what I plan to do to her and with her, but I don't want to break her delicate trust. I need to find some way to prepare her for what's coming, without breaking my contract with The Dungeon. I need her *with* me. She seems to me like a butterfly, pushing it's way out of its cocoon. But if I try to help her break free, she might not make it. Her wings are still far too fragile for the bumbling of a human's touch.

She's silent as I continue to use a low and soothing voice,

as though I were trying to gentle a wild cat. There is nothing wild in her in this moment. She's so far removed from the woman who threw a vase at me and ran away, risking the dark forest over me. Now she seems willing to risk kneeling at my feet and waiting for my commands—a whole other kind of forest with a whole other set of creatures which may devour her, body, mind, and soul.

"Deep down, we both know that while you may somehow be pure on the surface... underneath it all, in the depths, you are as dark as I am. You are a filthy wanton whore."

She flinches at this description. And who can blame her? What woman wants to be called a whore? Particularly one who hasn't even parted her thighs for the first man yet. It's as though I'm proclaiming her fortune rather than referencing her past. I'm declaring her destiny—or maybe telling her without telling her what I plan to do and pretending it's somehow just in her DNA to do it.

"I didn't say it was a bad thing. What if that word didn't carry the judgment? What if it was just a statement of the facts? What if it was no more consequential than preferring one type of chocolate over another? Tell, me, Macy... in the dark recesses of your mind, in your fantasies when you touch yourself... how many men are you with? If you lie to me, I'll know."

She blushes furiously, as only a redhead can do. "I-I can't..." is all she says.

I grip her by the hair and angle her face up to mine so she'll stop using these submissive gestures to hide from me. "You *can*."

She may have fantasies that mirror my own but she is not weak, so these demure gestures of obedience don't fool me. In fact, they're starting to grate on me. They make me want to punish her for this pretense. I haven't done a single thing to have her in such a state of submission. Not once, outside of that one day in the dungeon—which she liked— have I physically raised a hand to her.

She shakes her head, her jaw set. There it is—the evidence that she isn't so agreeable. My fierce little librarian.

"Tell me," I demand.

# 23

## MACY

My heart flutters so fast in my chest. I can't tell him this. I'm not sure why exactly I can't tell him. Am I afraid he'll judge me? Punish me? Am I afraid it'll make him feel he has permission to pass me around just because of what I fantasize about? Fantasies aren't consent.

I know full well that my fantasies don't mean I literally want to do all these things in real life or be treated this way. And yet Colin's very existence and the situation I've somehow fallen into, excite me in ways I didn't think possible. It's so far above the fantasy that I can't bring myself to fantasize anymore. The fantasy is too pale of a comparison to everything Colin is in reality. The way he makes me feel, what his mere presence does to my body. I've never felt things like this before, not even around Soren.

The big question that looms before me now is am I really that woman from my imagination? Or is she only a mirage? I'm terrified to admit to these things only to discover the reality isn't my fantasy, but my nightmare. And then I'm stuck, and I'll blame myself forever. My body trusts

Colin implicitly, like some scraggly little tail-wagging puppy who will happily follow his master off a cliff.

My mind rebels at this, but when he puts his hands on me, I'm powerless. I find myself sinking into the soft peace of his touch, the way his fingertips brush lightly against my skin, the way he touches my hair, the pleasure I remember his tongue bringing me between my legs. That moment feels like a lifetime ago.

"Mrs. Black?" His tone is like a prosecutor in a courtroom, and I feel incapable of perjury—as if there might be a legal punishment for lying to Colin.

"I don't remember exactly," I hedge.

"Estimate."

"Sometimes five, sometimes ten. I don't know, sometimes it's all blurry." This is so far from the truth. There is no blurry. There is no *random, faceless, I can't keep track of them* fantasy men. They are clear, and explicit. I can see the fabric of their crisp shirts, the sheen of the silk on their ties. But Colin doesn't question me further on it. He seems to accept my answer.

I let out a long, spiraling breath as I feel him move away from me. My gaze tracks him across the room to the exposed brick wall and the red leather sofa that sits against it. Colin sits in much the same way as he did on the plane. He crooks a finger, and I swallow hard.

I don't bother standing up, instead I crawl across the plush carpet. When I get to him, he reaches down between my legs, and I blush as he discovers just how wet I am.

He smirks. I move my hands to the zipper of his suit pants, assuming this is what he wants, a repeat performance of the plane, this time with more privacy. But he takes both of my hands in his and holds my gaze for a long moment.

"Straddle me."

I move to sit on his lap with one leg on either side of his

body, but he shifts me so that I'm straddling just one of his legs. Somehow this makes me blush harder than everything else so far today because I know what's coming.

He leans in and whispers, "Ride my leg until you come, little whore."

"I-I can't... I'll mess up your suit." A suit that no doubt cost multiple thousands of dollars.

"So, you'll mess up my suit," Colin says. "I have a closet full of them." He holds my gaze for a long moment. "Of course... you'll have to be punished for messing up my suit."

If I were smart I'd be scared of him, but maybe I'm just not all that smart. All the facts swirling around my head could never protect me from a man like Colin Black. There isn't a piece of knowledge I could possibly access that would help me right now. No library, no internet search could provide me with 'that one crazy trick...' that could help me now.

Colin doesn't hide his wealth. He doesn't try to play the Billionaire next door game, living in a middle class house, carrying a green card instead of black. But at the same time his wealth isn't loud or showy. It whispers. I adjust myself so that I'm straddling only one of his legs like he demanded, and I begin to grind against him.

He grips me by the shoulders, his mouth next to my ear. "That's a bad girl."

"Only because you want me to be," I retort.

He actually laughs out loud at this. I wonder if amusing him will reduce my punishment.

It takes a shockingly short amount of time for me to come, rutting against his leg like an animal in heat. He puts a hand over my mouth as I scream to muffle the sound. I'm not sure why. I already know he likes an audience, and we're underground anyway. No one can hear me scream. That thought should terrify me, but it only drives me.

He urges me onward until the last bits of pleasure have been wrung from me, then he pushes me back to the floor on my knees. Now I'm eye level with the mess I made.

He shakes his head in fake disappointment. "Clean it up."

I look at him blankly for a moment. Like does he want me to go get a wash cloth? I don't know the first thing about how to clean a suit... I feel like this is something I should have Googled at some point in my life but I can't even begin to imagine what the search phrase for this particular situation would be.

He holds my gaze and smirks. "I meant, with your tongue, Mrs. Black."

I blush.

Oh. Wow, I really am a virgin. Let us never speak of it.

I do as he asks, this humiliating, fucked-up thing which we both know is not improving the state of his suit. He strokes through my hair as I taste the evidence of my own pleasure.

After several minutes, his hand at the back of my neck stills me. "It's time for your punishment."

# 24

## MACY

I wake to the first full day of my honeymoon, alone. I knew this was how it would be, but still. I'm married, sort of. I'm on my honeymoon, and... I'm still a virgin. I must be cursed.

I trail a finger over the fresh cane welts Colin left on me in the dungeon last night. I'm not sure if the punishment was for messing up his suit or for the million tiny infractions he's probably been keeping track of in his head. Or maybe he just likes me marked like this. I can't honestly say that I hate it. There's a dark intimacy in these marks of possession that warm my flesh.

And afterward he dragged his tongue slowly over each one then made me come again with that same talented tongue. Then he put me to bed. I'd offered to return the favor, but he said... "I'll get what I need tomorrow night."

The sacrifice. My stomach flutters with nerves. Whatever the sacrifice is, it's happening tonight.

I'm still very aware of the fact that Livia thinks I'm on my honeymoon with William. I can't believe it was just two days ago that I stood in a church and promised to love and cherish Will through sickness and health, til death do us part. Or until the unfiled paperwork gets thrown in the honeymoon suite fire. Whichever.

I can't think which thing would be worse: For Livia to know that I'm actually with Colin—his more-or-less kidnapped bride—or to labor under the delusion that I'm closing my eyes and thinking of England with Will.

I know Colin has used a lot of restraint with me. I can see in his eyes that there's so much he wants to do with me, and yet he holds himself back. I could pretend I don't know why but I do know why. Haven't I had this same fantasy about a thousand times? Whatever is planned, he wants me as untouched as possible. I'm starting to think this may be the true reason he stayed away so long, because he knew he wouldn't have the self control otherwise. I know that sounds somewhat arrogant but virgin or not, I'm not stupid. I can see the lust burning in his eyes. No way does a man like Colin want a woman that much and not take what he wants unless there's a larger plan in place.

I just don't fully understand the purpose for that plan.

If Colin were another man, I could assume it was honor that restrained him. But after kidnapping and surveillance, those character traits are pretty much off the table.

It's ten in the morning and I haven't heard from him. Would he leave me alone in Dayne's cottage on our honeymoon? I take a quick shower and put on a pair of jeans and a T-shirt, then work to tame my dark red curls so I can get my hair into a ponytail.

I've tried using a straightening iron but when I put my hair in a ponytail after that I look like I'm time traveling and going to the disco.

When I get downstairs, I'm surprised to find Colin sitting at the table, reading a paper, and drinking coffee. There's a big spread of brunch food that was clearly delivered from the main kitchen at the resort.

"Did you sleep well?" he asks, not looking up from his paper.

"Yes."

I pour a cup of coffee and sit down.

"I thought you didn't drink coffee," he says looking at me like he's caught me in a gigantic lie.

"I don't, but..." I trail off because I'm not about to tell him I need something stronger than tea to cope with my jangled nerves and figure out what the hell I feel about anything, if I should be trying to escape or not, what the possible consequences of *that* might be, along with about a hundred thoughts I haven't properly filed and categorized yet, and whiskey is way too big of a leap for me right now. So coffee, it is.

The heated way he looks at me, I swear any moment he'll just take me over the kitchen counter, but he doesn't.

Will things feel normal between us after whatever he has planned for me tonight? Is there a way anything can be normal between us given the nature of our relationship and how it started? *Do* we have a relationship?

Colin stands abruptly. My gaze goes to his pants to see the tell-tale signs of his erection. Yes, he definitely wants me, but he makes no move to touch me, nor does he make any request for me to take care of his needs.

"I have some business to take care of. The kitchen is fully stocked. I'll see you tonight."

And then he's gone. Something in my chest tightens, worried the business he has to take care of is his raging erection and that he doesn't plan to just use his hand.

I spend most of the day pacing around the house like a caged animal. I can leave and wander the grounds but it should be no mystery why I'm not too excited to wander unescorted around a place called The Dungeon.

Jeffrey is staying at the main resort, and it's too quiet. Once again I think about escaping. Is Colin giving me that out? But no, he never removed the tracking bracelet. He could still find me and drag me back. Is this some sort of bizarre loyalty test?

I think about running but I'm too curious about tonight. I know it's stupid. What if whatever's happening will be horrible? What if it traumatizes me? What if it's painful or... but I'm just too curious. I just need to know. And so I waffle on whether or not to run or stay.

I pace the house. I eat the food set aside in the kitchen, and I wait for the sun to make it's journey across the sky and bring us to night.

It's almost sunset when I go upstairs to my bathroom. I find a note on the counter with bathing instructions. He's left a small bottle of champagne for me, along with candles and rose petals and fragrant vanilla oil. So I follow his instructions, and take a bath with candles and champagne in the bath oil.

A white dress is waiting for me on the bed when I get out, and Colin stands there, dressed in a suit. He doesn't speak a word to me as I drop the towel. His dark eyes drink me in, but still he doesn't take what's his to devour.

"Get dressed."

There's no bra and panties, only the dress. It's long and flowy, like a much simpler wedding gown, but no veil or flowers. No train at the back. I put on the dress and the gold heels. He pulls a key from his pocket and unlocks and removes the bracelet from my wrist.

"Just for tonight," he says. Then he guides me downstairs.

While I was in the bath, room service was delivered to

the cottage. The table is set with a white linen table cloth. A light honey scent wafts from the beeswax candles. Dinner is a chicken and vegetable dish over noodles in some sort of white sauce and white wine—all things relatively safe to eat while wearing a white dress.

He doesn't say a single word to me, and I can't bring myself to say anything either. I want to ask what's going to happen. I want to ask him anything, but I can't find any words to speak. That's a Macy Miracle. I can always find something to talk about, but even my nervous chatter doesn't make an appearance right now. Everything feels too heavy for words.

Does he *want* to do whatever's about to happen?

Finally I do find words. "Master? Will I be safe?"

His dark gaze holds mine for nearly a full minute, and he nods.

I let out the breath I didn't know I'd been holding. For some reason I believe him. Maybe I shouldn't. Why should I believe a man with probably no internal compass?

We finish dinner. He stands, snuffs out the candles, and offers me his hand. I take it like the absolute fool I am, and allow him to lead me to whatever fate is planned.

# 25

## MACY

I 'm inside the fantasy now. No longer am I separate from the visions and images that drifted by each morning for years on rotation... the private porn library of my mind. Now I *am* her. I am that woman, about to be taken for the first time in a room full of strangers.

In a bizarre way, this feels like our wedding, the thing that actually binds us. A contract isn't a ceremony, and we didn't get the ceremony. I think the only thing Colin is capable of promising me is that he'll never let me go. And now like some queen of the dark ages, I have an audience for the consummation of an arranged marriage to a powerful man whose word is law.

Colin stands beside me, his hand in mine, near the entrance. No one has noticed us yet. For the moment we blend into the rest of the group. His hand feels warm and solid wrapped around mine. It doesn't escape me, especially given the environment that we're in and the ways various couples are engaging, that he could hold me by the arm like a prisoner, or by the scruff of the neck like some dog. But instead, his fingers are laced with mine. It's somehow reassuring.

My heart hammers in my chest, and all I know is that somehow tonight I'm the main event. I take a slow breath to steady myself and calm my nerves. I don't know why I haven't run from him, why I haven't struggled. It seems obvious to me that these people are here willingly. I've been made aware of the contracts that get signed before people come into this space. They aren't a thousand pages, they are a single page with very clearly spelled out rules in a readable big font. Nothing can be mistaken. There's no fine print here. So if I screamed and begged for help, I'm pretty sure, someone would help me. I think. Okay I'm not completely sure, but it seems like everyone's agreement is really important here, so it's hard to imagine they'd all be okay with me being here against my will.

And, I didn't sign anything. Colin signed something, but some understanding or awareness passed between him and the people at the door with the contracts, and I didn't sign anything. What does that mean? Does it mean my desires and consent don't matter? Or is it protecting me from being bound by some rules I might not want to be bound to?

I'm really not sure. Colin's touch still inspires the same stupid trust it has from the first time his hand rested against my throat. Against all reason I trust he'll keep me safe. I don't want to scream or fight because I'm so close to getting to have my fantasy come to life, and I want to let it play out. I don't know how or why I'm sure, but I'm *sure* if I were in true distress, Colin would protect me. He'd do whatever it took.

I turn my attention back to our surroundings. There's a stage off to the side with musicians; it's large, but it isn't the focal point of the room. I hear slow deep drumbeats along with other percussive noises... a tap tap tap tap, lighter than the drum beat, like an animal bone being struck against another animal bone. It's like we've traveled back to a time where everything is life and death and nature cycling and spiraling endlessly around us with no other complications.

It's mostly dark with no electric light—only candlelight. All the flames are contained and protected. There are maybe a hundred people in this room, and we wouldn't want to create a fire hazard. There's a large semi-circle multi-level elevated platform set up like an amphitheater, so everyone can watch the same activity in the middle of the room without having their view obstructed. Some people are already milling around on the different levels, choosing the vantage point from which they'll watch.

Along the wall, near the stage with the musicians is another elevated platform, a second, smaller stage. There are three regal-looking chairs up there and I see Dayne, Soren, and Griffin. Livia's men. Dayne stands in the middle, the other two sit in the outermost chairs.

My face flames. I don't know what I expected but I didn't expect to see Dayne, Soren, and Griffin here. I thought they'd be back home. After all, they were at the wedding. It never occurred to me they might get on their own jet to come to Costa Rica. Did Soren know this was happening when he first delivered me to Colin? Is *this* what he meant by me being a sacrifice? But no, this can't be the thing keeping his stock prices up.

Before I can ask myself further questions, the music stops for a moment and a spotlight lands on Dayne. Silence falls over the room. Finally, when the tension and anticipation reaches its zenith, he speaks.

"As you all know, when you enter this space with a toy, you must share with everyone. Consent to step into this space is consent to play or be played with by anyone here. The one exception has always been the gold collar. My collar. In the past this collar has been reserved only for myself with my own toys, the women I didn't wish to share here because it *is* my club."

The room fills with polite chuckles.

Dayne continues. "Now that collar is worn exclusively by my wife, Livia."

I look around, but I don't see my best friend, something I'm ridiculously grateful for. Whatever's about to happen, I think I could stand for her men to watch it—after all, Soren has featured in my fantasies about a million times in just that capacity. But Livia? Yeah, no, I'm not there yet. Maybe never. Dayne continues.

"Starting tonight, there will be a new exclusive level of membership in the dungeon called The Silver Circle. Silver Circle membership will be by invitation only, so don't ask. Griffin, Soren, and myself will decide who we wish to include. The steep annual membership includes private events only for members and the right to control who gets to play with your pet inside the dungeon whenever you're here. Initiates must participate in a public ritual and present a virgin sacrifice."

A gasp rises from the crowd, and this time Dayne chuckles.

"I know, it's so rare to find a virgin anything. The sacrifice must be at least 21 years old and here of her own free will." I feel like Dayne looks directly at me when he says this. Colin's hand squeezes mine tighter as though he fears I might run away.

I hear murmurs as people make quips like "Good luck with that." I imagine the numbers of women who've reached twenty-one without deflowering are a pretty small group, something which makes me feel like an even greater freak at almost thirty. No one here seems too troubled by the term sacrifice. So either they all understand this is somehow symbolic or they're all closet serial killers. I'm hoping it's the former. I'm 99.999% sure that Colin isn't planning to murder me just to be part of this stupid Silver Circle thing, and Dayne did mention free will. Nobody is volunteering for that kind of sacrifice.

Dayne clears his throat, and the crowd settles down. "The Silver Circle gives members in this exclusive level the right to use of a silver collar in the dungeon which entitles them to share the woman wearing it only with those of his choosing and no one else. It carries the same weight and authority as my gold collar. Anyone who doesn't respect the rights of the silver collar, will be blacklisted from the dungeon for life."

Dayne keeps talking, but I don't hear the rest because Colin has bent to speak low in my ear. "Do you understand why you're here now?"

His nearness and rumbling voice against my skin has such a strong effect on me. I've gone to great pains to not make it obvious how strongly I want this man, even though there are a million reasons why that's probably the stupidest desire I could entertain.

Colin's mouth remains next to my ear as he continues. "I like sharing my toys, but I want to call the shots. I plan to bring you to the dungeon often, and I don't intend to be held to the rules of sharing."

It's kind of... sweet, in a Colin way. And it occurs to me that the entire Silver Circle was probably created to accommodate his desire to control who he shares me with. Though maybe Dayne, Soren, and Griffin don't like the idea of me being shared indiscriminately either, given that they know exactly how I came to belong to Mr. Black.

Colin leans close to me again and whispers, "I selected the men who will be involved tonight."

"What's going to happen?" I finally have the nerve to ask

this. I've wanted to ask it since the moment I knew *something* would be happening. But I was afraid to know.

"I can't tell you. You'll be given the option to go forward or say no."

"And if I say no?" I turn again to face him. His expression is unreadable.

Finally he says: "As my wife, you'll be accompanying me here. So unless you want to have to sleep with anyone who happens to be in the room at the time, it's in your interest to be the sacrifice. No one will fuck you but me tonight, that's the one thing I can promise."

My breath catches as it comes into sharper focus that very soon I'll lose my virginity in front of a live audience. I always knew this, but it's only now really hitting me. If feels somehow as though everything in my life has been culminating to this moment of consummation.

The response I should have to his proclamation of what's to come is horror, shame, terror. I should want to escape. I run through my options now. What happens if I say no? Yes, he says he'll bring me here again and then my options will be gone, but... no because I'd have to sign the contract to get into this room.

Could he make me do that? It seems there are strong rules here to keep everybody and everything above boards legally. Dayne wouldn't want his club to get shut down. I'm not sure what the laws are in Costa Rica, but it still seems important that everyone involved has given consent, and coercion isn't consent. Would he just play with someone else if I refused? That bothers me more.

As I stand here I'm angry. I live in a constant war with myself—the battle between how I'm supposed to feel and react to things, versus how I actually do feel. The things I'm supposed to want and not want, versus the things I actually desire. The fight over the rightness and wrongness of things.

The politics of things. The free will or lack thereof. The possible coercion. What society thinks, what other people think. It all rolls over me in an attempt to steal my true will and desire, to subjugate me into a family-friendly version of myself, something appropriate for mass consumption.

I've played this up with my bookish ways, weird facts, and nerd glasses. And of course these freckles. God, the freckles. People see freckles and assume innocence. There is no known seductress in the history of the world with curly auburn hair, and freckles. And so I've played into this image, this character that people feel most comfortable with, this girl everyone else wants me to be.

It's not that I'm not those things, but somewhere inside me I know I'm more, if only I could set her free.

Is there a single choice in life we get to make that is one hundred percent free of coercion, manipulation, or someone else's viewpoint shoehorned into our minds when we're too young to fight back? How much of me is a separate complete thing, and how much is a collection of experiences and other people's ideas? I just want to be free and be the version of me that's locked tightly inside my mind, never able to fully express herself because of other people's oppressive opinions about what is and isn't okay to feel, do, or be in this world.

And how the fuck do they know? Who died and made them god? Who gave them authority over my life or internal processing? When did it occur that anyone but me had the right to live my life? I'm the one who faces the consequences of my life. It's no one's business but my own.

And yet...

I feel stuck in an endless limbo where the only other person on the battlefield is another version of myself. There is the me I want to be lined up against what's socially accept-able, politically correct, expected, normal, nice. That polite unoffensive me is the one loaded down with all the weapons, handed to her via *other people's opinions and moral judgments*, other people's busybodying. Aren't they kept busy enough with their own lives? If only they spent half so much energy on themselves.

I'm not supposed to want to do this with Colin. I'm not supposed to want to lose my virginity in this way. My mind fights and rails and screams, but my body says yes. Of the two me's on the battlefield, the real me is what my body wants. My simple, primal desires beneath the lie of everyone else's story, even beneath the lie of my own story.

Suddenly there's a shift in the crowd as attention is pulled to me and Colin. People start to notice us, and I feel Colin's hand on my back as he leads me forward. A soft spotlight shines down on the center of the room, and I'm back in the fantasy only this time it's real. And instead of imagining and pretending, I am finally doing and to hell with a world that tells me I can't.

My mind flashes to my dark book group... "I would never do that..." "She barely tried to escape..." "It's so unbelievable..." "If it were me I would..."

I squeeze my eyes shut for a moment to block out all that fucking stupidity. Who the fuck cares what they would do? This is MY story.

I feel the change come over me, as though I'm a shapeshifter in the forest, and I have the realization that this actually *is* the full moon. I caught a glimpse of it when we were walking from the cottage to the main building earlier, but I didn't allow myself to process it, to give it too much weight. Desire prickles over my senses. It feels like a wave of fire licking over me, burning away the parts of me that hid behind the other parts of me society would find acceptable and normal.

I spent months jealous of Livia, that she got these three

hot kinky men, that she got to surrender in this way and have pleasure without the shame and without the guilt. And here I am, in this room. Somehow I have brought this fantasy to myself. I'm not the victim here so don't you dare frame me that way.

I manifested this. I called this up from the aether. I added magic to it every single morning in the ritual of my orgasm, and now I'm claiming what I sent out into the universe because it's mine, and no one has to understand that but me. I don't know what I think about the reality of Colin, but I know what I feel about this moment. I'm not a sacrifice. A sacrifice is something demanded. It's an obligation. It's forced or coerced. It's something done to you. But I am not a sacrifice. I'm a willing participant. The real sacrifice was all the time I've lied and run from myself. All the time I've wasted standing in somebody else's truth.

I stand in the middle of the room under the spotlight. There's a large round table with white leather upholstery.

Dayne speaks again, and this time it's to Colin. "Is this your offering?" he asks, indicating me.

"It is."

Dayne turns to me then. "Take your opportunity to leave this place, Macy."

It's jarring to hear him speak my name in a place that feels like I should be anonymous. Colin's hand squeezes mine again. I don't think he realizes he's doing it.

"No. I'm staying," I say.

Is Dayne trying to save me? Is he trying to go against the agreement between Soren and Colin? The agreement he had to have signed off on? Or was he going along, and now he's having second thoughts? A guilty conscience? Was he watching me? Did he witness my internal war just now? Is he, like so many others, trying to save me from a struggle that wouldn't exist without their judgment?

I note an angry expression on Soren's face and am sure if I had the nerve to look at Colin I'd see the same anger. Yes, Dayne is going off script.

"Macy, do you understand what's going to happen here tonight? Multiple men will touch you. You'll be laid out like a sacrifice, and your virginity will be taken in front of a crowd of strangers. You should leave. I will protect you."

Does he not understand that Colin won't release me either way? Dayne's protection only extends to his club. Maybe he could demand Colin release me if Colin wants use of the club, but I have a feeling he'd choose to keep me over his membership.

I feel the fury surge through me like a wave of electricity. If my hair were literally on fire right now, I wouldn't be surprised. Of all people, someone who owns a place like this judging me and what I can handle and deciding what's best for me and what I should want...

"NO! I know what I'm doing."

Dayne looks shocked. He actually reels back, as though I've slapped him, or as though the power of that definitive no, actually caused his head to snap back.

Indistinct murmurs rise up around us, and I know the people here also realize Dayne isn't following whatever script was laid out. Or perhaps it's the shock of someone yelling at Dayne when all anyone seems to show him is the greatest deference. Oh, the intrigue.

His expression is inscrutable as he stares down at me. It's so strange to me that it's Dayne and not Soren holding this role. Though Soren never would have tried to save me— something I strangely respect. A part of me may hate the man Soren is, but I respect that he hasn't treated me like a helpless child in need of shielding. Finally, Dayne sighs and nods.

The drumbeats start again from the stage.

Then it's Colin who speaks. "I offer, my wife, Macy Black, as a sacrifice to the dungeon in exchange for founding membership in The Silver Circle."

There's a unified gasp from the room, and I'm pretty sure it's the *wife* part that's throwing them. I feel strangely giddy he presented me in this way as his wife. Not his slut, pet, whore, toy, concubine... his wife.

He guides me to the table and helps me onto it. The zipper for the dress is on the side, he pulls it down, and I think he's about to undress me in front of the curious crowd, but instead someone passes him a white sheet. He unfolds it and drapes it over me before helping me out of the dress. The sheet continues to keep me veiled from hungry eyes who have forgotten how all this started and are now interested in watching the scene unfold before them like any of a million twisted kinky games played out in this room before tonight.

Colin fades back into the shadows and several men all dressed formally as though they should be at a fundraising gala step into the light. With the tribal drum beats going deeper and louder, I'd expect something dramatic like black cloaks or raw nudity, but the suit thing is a Colin thing and I can't help but feel this is his vision as much as Soren's.

I count nine men, and they each take a place around this large table. My body laid out before them only covers a very small part of the space. You could lay eight other women out on this table all spaced apart like numbers on a clock.

They aren't wearing masks. If any of them were convicted criminals I could probably pick them out of a lineup or a book of mugshots, but none of them seems worried about this possibility, which tells me they're all squeaky clean officially and that even with their faces uncovered, they remain truly anonymous to me.

They're all attractive, and it occurs to me that Colin

picked men who any sane woman would *want* to have touch them. No one creepy or gross or slovenly. Any one of these men is the kind of man women would viciously compete for the attentions of; and tonight, all their attention is on me.

No one speaks. Aside from the initial talk, there doesn't seem to be planned narration for this ritual. The first man approaches. He holds two black boxes, the smaller stacked on top. He places these boxes without comment on the table.

The drumming intensifies.

Then the first stranger's hands are on me. He skims gently over my body, touching me through the sheet, but never directly touching my skin. He strokes and fondles my breasts. My nipples grow erect in response to this attention, poking through the sheet, clearly visible. He leans over me and kisses me on the mouth.

I moan into him, my inhibitions scattering away. He rises and stretches my hands over my head, enclosing them in gleaming silver cuffs attached to the table. He strokes my hair and the side of my throat. My hips arch up to meet his hands as they move farther down, between my legs, stroking my warming core.

He massages and strokes but he never goes beneath the sheet. His hands never stray to my bare flesh. I understand implicitly, that's for Colin. The stranger continues until I realize he isn't going to stop until I come. This isn't just some symbolic gesture.

And then I blush as I realize that I'm expected to come for all of them with all these onlookers even before anyone sees an inch of my nudity or any actual sex occurs.

I close my eyes and a moment later I hear Colin's voice in my ear, urging me on. "Come for him."

Was I waiting for this permission?

I let go, accepting the pleasure on offer, my body writhing under the sheet as I grind against the stranger's hand. When the first man has finished, taking nothing for himself, the table is rotated to the next. This process happens nine times. Each man claims my mouth, demanding I open to his kiss. The only part of his body allowed to plunge inside any part of mine is his tongue, and only my mouth. They each stroke my hair, and my throat, my breasts over the sheet, and between my legs. I give them each my pleasure as Colin demanded, as the drumming goes on, and the voyeurs watching this display seem to disappear into the background with each orgasm until I feel alone in the spotlight with these men.

By the time they're all finished, the sheet is soaked with a giant wet spot, visible to all who watched. It's clear I didn't fake my pleasure. It wasn't just a show. And still, I'm so turned on because Colin is next.

I open my eyes when he approaches. I'd expected the men to move back into the crowd but they've just shifted to make space for Colin at the table. He uncuffs my wrists. The first guy takes the two boxes from the center of the table and holds them as Colin spreads the sheet out over the center of the table.

He guides me to lay back on it, spreading my legs wide. Nothing shields me now from the men who touched me or our larger audience. I swallow hard as Colin loosens and removes his tie, his gaze never leaving mine. I expect him to take something else off, but he doesn't, not for this show because it's not about him.

He takes the smallest of the black boxes and opens it, revealing my wedding ring. He holds out a hand, demanding mine. I offer him my left hand, and he slides the ring on my finger. And somehow, this twisted fucked-up moment feels like my real wedding. Not the moment in the church with Will, not the signing of the contract, but this moment.

He unzips his pants, freeing his cock as he leans over me. "And now, Mrs. Black, I'm finally taking what's mine."

He shoves into me so fast I don't have time to process the pain, and somehow I know that was for my benefit. The *rip the band-aid off fast* approach. Once he's broken through my barrier, he goes still, waiting for me to adjust to him. I arch my hips up in invitation, and he begins to move, slowly rocking into me, as he cradles my body against him. More shocking than the public way this is unfolding, is his unexpected tenderness.

The drumbeats and light and people all seem to go away, and it feels like we're alone in the dark. I've never thought it was realistic to expect a virgin to have an orgasm from her first time, but my body has been so primed from nine other orgasms, that I'm on the edge again as he drives into me harder. I claw at his shoulders, trying to hold on as I buck wildly beneath him.

I'm not sure who is fucking who, but finally my pleasure crests over me in a wave, and then Colin is spilling his seed into me. He holds me tight against him as he thrusts until the act is complete. As he withdraws, my awareness slowly returns to the room. The audience, the men standing around the table, the drumming, and finally Colin's possessive gaze like an animal who just marked his territory.

He picks up the second black box and opens it to reveal the silver collar.

I distantly hear Dayne speak again. "Colin Black, The Dungeon welcomes you to The Silver Circle."

The engraving on the outside of the collar reads: "Property of Colin Black. Touch only with permission." He unlocks it and slips it around my throat.

Polite applause breaks out into the space as though we just performed a symphony instead of a sex act.

As Colin helps me up, I glance back at the table. The white sheet has my blood on it, evidence that Colin has indeed produced a virgin for this event. It's taking all my willpower not to mentally ramble about the fact that you can be a virgin and not bleed, but I guess it doesn't matter now. I bled, and now Colin's in the inner circle.

He wraps the sheet around me, picks me up, and carries me out of the ballroom.

# 26

## MACY

I wake and glance over at the alarm clock. The red numbers read 2:33. I'm in Colin's bed, but I'm alone again. The house feels empty. I push back the blankets and get out of bed, grabbing the silk robe off a nearby chair. After he took my virginity in the hottest, most fucked-up expression of my own twisted fantasies, he brought me back to the cottage.

He fed me champagne and strawberries and put me in a bubble bath with candles to relax. When I got out of the tub he gave me an ornately wrapped gift. Black paper, white satin ribbon. Inside the box was lingerie. Not just any lingerie. It wasn't kinky or dirty. It wasn't revealing. It was classy and the most expensive lingerie that has ever been on my body.

I knew it was expensive, not because it was silk, but because it was La Perla. The long white silk gown with pale gold frastaglio embroidery, and the matching robe with the same detailing at the sleeves and hem. It was several thousand dollars... for sleepwear. I only know this because Livia has some of their lingerie and was looking through their website the last time I was at her house. My eyes nearly bugged out at the prices.

So now, I'm wandering through this giant misnamed cottage, wearing lingerie several times more expensive than my first car, looking for my husband. There is a pang of unfamiliar fear low in my belly. For the first time I'm worried... what if he's cheating on me? On our honeymoon.

I didn't sit and worry about this before, but now that he's taken what he wants from me... and the mystery is gone, there's a part of me that fears this is when it starts, the sneaking around.

Maybe Colin is sharing some woman with Jeffrey at the main resort. If he's sharing me, doesn't he expect me to share him? I know it's not fair, but I don't care. I don't want to share him with other women. I shouldn't want to be with him at all, but now that I am, I want him to be mine, not just for me to be his.

I stare down at the gold band on my finger as I make my way through the dimly lit hallway. It's quieter than a tomb. The main level is much the same, but darker. A few lights from the pool outside shine in through the windows, along with light from the full moon.

It's a sort of funny coincidence. Don't sacrifices happen on the full moon? In stories? What are the odds that my wedding would just happen to coincide with the growing moon and that the night of this ritual deflowering would occur when it officially reached fullness? Maybe it was planned this way, though I chose the wedding date. Maybe it was fate.

I run my hand over my abdomen. I can't believe I didn't realize when it was. I'm one of those women with an obnoxiously regular cycle and almost no symptoms of any kind. And, I'm in sync with the moon. The only symptom I get is a low warm twinge when I'm ovulating. I feel that low twinge now and I realize what this means. Leave it to me to get pregnant the first time I have sex. I'm at the peak of my fertility standing in the moonlight, feeling the evidence of this truth, possibly carrying my captor husband's child, and he's what? Already bored with me? Already fucking another woman somewhere?

I swipe at the tears. No, this isn't my fairy tale. Or maybe it's how all the fairy tales go. After all, they all seem to end at the wedding, don't they? We don't know that the princess is really happy forever, or how short this *forever* might actually be.

Every Disney princess that I watched as a little girl now feels like a lie as I imagine all the princes slinking around with a parade of women behind the princesses' back, while she sits alone in the castle getting fat with his child.

Part of me wants to go back upstairs and just pretend I didn't wake up to an empty bed. When I fell asleep he had me pressed against his body. He didn't even try to fuck me again. He put me in the lingerie and put me to bed. It felt sweet at the time. But now it feels like boredom, his boredom.

I'm about to go back upstairs when I notice a small sliver of light coming from the dungeon. Does he have a woman down there? I don't know why it should bother me that he might tie another woman up, that he might spank her, that he might demand a title from her—Master or Sir. Of all things to be jealous and upset about, this seems the most ridiculous.

I'm suddenly filled with rage. I can almost feel my hair glow with it, as though I carry some arcane power of fury in my red hair. I feel like I could eviscerate this man with my glare alone. Who does he think he is? Fuck him. I'm going to go down there and I'm going to scream at this motherfucker.

What's he going to do? Kill me? He went to far too much trouble for me for that. Right?

There's a ninety-nine percent chance that he set off a chain of events tonight that will result in me carrying his child. Is he going to risk that? My contract *did* explicitly call for heirs after all. So I know he wants kids. What's the motherfucker going to do?

I fling the door open and fly down the stairs like a banshee about to start shrieking, when I hear a voice and stop short. I'm in a bricked-in stairwell. He hasn't seen me, and I don't think he's heard me yet. I'm two steps from the bottom. If I'd taken one more step, I'm sure in my flurrying rush that the silk gown would have flashed around the edges of the brick wall, revealing my presence if he happened to glance that way.

The voice I heard wasn't Colin's, and it wasn't a woman. I hold my breath wondering if I can ease back up the stairs even as I feel compelled to stay and eavesdrop.

"P-please. Please Mr. Black. I'm sorry. I'm so sorry."

"Are you?" Colin's voice comes out darker and more terrifying than I've ever heard it. He sounds like the angel of death, and I know with striking clarity that this man isn't getting out of this basement.

"I'm on the board!" he says.

"We'll vote on a new member when you don't show up for the next meeting."

"B-but... they'll ask questions."

"Will they? Costa Rica is a dangerous place. When they finally find your body it will no doubt be mauled beyond recognition. You were known to go off on dangerous adventures alone without a guide."

I can't explain his voice right now. It's dark and terrifying but so deceptively calm. It's like he's still, peaceful inside as the storm and terror rages around him, as it emits from him to destroy everyone and everything in his path. But he remains untouched by all of it.

Colin continues. "Anyway, I think the board will be distracted at our next meeting. I plan for Mrs. Black to be carrying my child by then, and you know what that means."

I don't even know what that means, but my hand goes to my stomach protectively wondering which is worse, a boy or a girl? Which gender is safest from whatever Colin is? How could I ever protect my child from this man? I've known deep down that he's a killer, and somewhere in my head I fluffed it off as though I were watching a movie and not living my actual life—as though there were no actual consequences for the truth of what he is.

The reality sinks in now that there may be a third person to worry about. Not just me.

"I-I didn't think you knew."

"You don't think I know when people betray me? Are you trying to insult me, Jack?"

"If you knew why would you let me touch her tonight?"

This man, Jack, was at the sacrifice. He was one of the men that touched me before Colin... I squeeze my eyes shut trying to block the memories out because I know how my body will react to them, and not in any kind of appropriate way considering the even darker turn the night is taking.

"What better way to get you alone? Over a hundred people witnessed you touch Mrs. Black tonight. They know I chose everyone. Why would I let a man I intended to kill touch my wife? You think you're the only person who discounted that possibility? And you knew you were guilty of betraying me. Nobody else does. Nobody betrays me, and you knew that. You're off the radar in the middle of nowhere. Everyone is distracted by alcohol, drugs, and sex. I think it's perfect. Don't you, Mrs. Black?"

I freeze in the stairwell. Oh god. He knows I'm here. Oh

god. Oh god. Oh god. I'm no longer as cavalier and brave as I was two seconds ago. I'm no longer convinced he won't just kill me, too. Can't anyone be his breeding stock? Am I more dangerous than I am valuable to him alive?

"Macy, I know you're there. I have ears like a wolf. You think you can run down those stairs, and I won't hear it?"

Why didn't the other guy hear it? But I know why. He's focused on whatever weapon Colin has. His entire life is narrowed down to the power wielded over him. I know that feeling very well, except I knew it wasn't going to end in my untimely death. Except now I'm not so sure.

"Macy. Come. Here."

I breathe deeply and take the last two steps down into the dungeon. I'm surprised by all the plastic lining the walls and the floor underneath them. It stretches so far, I'm standing on it, the plastic crinkling under my bare feet.

Of course he can't get blood on the carpet. Seriously, who carpets a dungeon? In all my innocence, even I have enough sense to see that.

In spite of this fucked-up situation, I blush as I see one of the men who touched me tonight—the first one to touch me. He's so handsome and about Colin's age. He's tied to a chair under a spotlight in the middle of the room. It's all very cinematic. Colin stands over him holding a large knife, looking crazed like a horror movie monster.

He stares at me, daring me to run from him right now.

"C-Colin..."

He raises a brow... "You really think this is the time to be on a first name basis? You know what I want from you, especially when you know you've been a very bad girl."

"M-Master," I breathe.

How the fuck can he play a sex game at a time like this? Though I think I've always known, it was never just a sex game with Colin. He genuinely and truly sees me as his property. Something clenches inside me at this. I have fantasies, yes. I'm attracted, yes. He can provide all sorts of things for me, but I want to be loved. I want to be seen. I want someone who is truly *with* me. I want someone I'm safe with.

"Please don't do this. Don't hurt him," I say.

"I think you're *really* scared I'll hurt *you*. You don't know this man. What is he to you?"

"He's a human being!" I want to add: *you psycho*, but that might be a little much, and I don't want to taunt the psycho with the knife. The psycho that is my husband and may be the father of my child.

The concept of a human being doesn't seem to register with Colin. It's as though no one but him is really real. Everyone is a means to an end. Or a prop. Or a plot point in his story. Or a scripted character in his game. There is no light of recognition that killing this man affects his world in any meaningful way.

The tears stream down my cheeks. "Please don't do this."

"If you knew what he did, you'd support me."

"Don't listen to him," Jack says. "He's a liar. He's a sociopath. Can't you see?"

"Yes, him standing over you with a giant knife was a big clue, Jack."

I can't believe I just said those words out loud, but I'm so stressed out right now. The adrenaline floods me. There's a ringing in my ears, and it's true, my biggest fear is that Colin gets a taste of blood, and I'm next. But if I can somehow stop him, then nothing really happened tonight, and he won't feel compelled to kill me too, to erase the witness because I'm not stupid enough to think he's attached enough to me to spare me if I've become a threat.

After all, he just let me go and stayed away for months

while I planned my sham wedding. He likes things to follow his script. And this is not following his script.

"Please, I'm sorry," I say, echoing Jack.

"What do you have to be sorry for?" Colin asks. He seems genuinely perplexed. Didn't he just tell me I was a bad girl? Did he mean for trying to stop him? Does he not care that I saw this? My mind races trying to figure out what any of it means.

"I should have stayed in my room." I back toward the stairs.

"I didn't say you could leave. Stay right there."

I stop, trying to assess my options, trying to figure out how each plays out. "Don't kill him."

"I can't let him go now. He'll talk. He'll destroy me. Or kill me. He might even hurt you."

"I won't! You can let me go!" Jack shouts, struggling to no avail in his ropes.

"Why would he hurt me? You're the one with the knife."

"He hurt my sister." Colin's words come out a growl.

Jack's eyes widen, and it's clear that he wasn't aware of something. "I thought this was because I fucked you on the Connors' account and voted against you on that thing at the board meeting last month..."

Colin leans down until he's an inch from his face. "My. Sister." He enunciates each word.

"She wanted it."

Colin backhands him hard enough the chair tilts back and he has to catch it before Jack falls.

"If you knew that, why the fuck would you let me touch her?" Jack says, his head tilting toward me. "Why would you let me be the *first*?"

I'm frozen to the spot. I don't know the exact details of what Jack did to Colin's sister, but I have ideas. And it doesn't exactly enshrine me as a woman Colin cares anything about.

If this man is a monster, why would Colin let him touch me? I shake that thought from my head. Colin's a monster, and I've been A-okay with *him* touching me this whole time.

Jack's chair faces toward me, he's reasoning with me with his eyes, willing me to see what I can already see. Colin let this monster touch me so as soon as he takes out the trash, I'm next. Colin stands behinds Jack, his eyes also on mine. Two men trying to communicate with me non-verbally and one of them is holding a knife.

Finally, Colin speaks. He's speaking to Jack, but he's still looking at me.

"When you turn up missing and then turn up dead, do you think anyone from this club would ever think I would know what you did to my sister and still let you touch my wife? Do you think that's even a thought a normal person could imagine? I closed, every. Fucking. Loophole. Motherfucker."

And with this final pronouncement, Colin swipes the knife clean across Jack's throat. There's a horrible gurgling sound, as way more blood than I could ever imagine comes bubbling out of this throat. I'm going to be sick.

Finally I come unfrozen from the spot, I turn and run up the stairs. As soon as I'm on the main floor, I rip the robe off and fling it away from me, I hike up the silk nightgown and flee into the night across manicured rolling lawn. Rich people and their fucking manicured lawns.

Do they get a manual or something the second they come into money? *Welcome to the Rich People club. All lawns forevermore that you possess shall be no taller than an inch and a half and perfectly plush, soft, and green. Any violation of this law shall be severely frowned upon and no more white parties for you.*

I can see better running this time, in the bright full moon. It's like everything has come full circle. The first time I ran into the night away from Colin, the moon was new and dark, now it's full and all has been illuminated. And if I don't escape him this time...

I can't think about that. I just keep running. Thunder cracks in the distance, but the storm feels far away.

"MACY!" Colin roars from the house. He sounds feral, like a wild animal. It's so loud and surreal, I'm sure he'll wake the entire resort, even though the main building is off in the distance. There's a lot of privacy and trees and rolling hills between the cottage and where all the people are, where safety is.

# 27

## COLIN

I'm covered in blood as I run after her, but I don't care. I can't let her get away with this knowledge inside her. My mind tries to intrude with thoughts about what I may have touched in the house chasing her. What trail of DNA or blood I may have left behind. What do I have to clean? Besides the body, what do I have to do to get things back on track?

I usually feel calm when I remove a problem, but right now I feel anything but calm. I don't know what I'll do when I catch her, but I have to catch her. I'm dimly aware that calling out to her in that insanely loud roar might not be the wisest thing to do. The resort is far away, it's the middle of the night, but still. I'm not following all my carefully crafted plans. I'm coloring outside the lines and it makes me feel... wrong.

It makes me feel unsure and unsafe, and I just have to get to her. She left her robe in the house, I nearly tripped over it lying in the middle of the floor as she fled out into the night. I wonder if she's ripped off the gown so she can run better. The thought of her running out here in the night naked, the thought that someone else could reach her and pin her down before me sends my adrenaline surging.

I resist the need to call her name again. The more I scream her name the more she knows how close I am. She knows I'm chasing, and I need some element of surprise. I didn't chase her the first night she ran. I don't know why. I knew there was nowhere she could go and I didn't have to get my hands dirty running her down, but this is different. She has a golden moment to escape.

And what will she say? Will she turn me in? Will she say I killed a man right in front of her? Will she tell them what I've done to her? Thunder rolls in the distance but it's getting closer, it's coming this way. I feel like the storm and I are one thing, and the more erratic I become, the faster and closer the storm moves. Could my own storm consume me? I have never once had this thought. I've always felt invincible. Before Macy.

So she's the problem. She's the one making me weak. *Eliminate the problem.* My mind screams it at me. It's the only way to put all the pieces back together again. It's the only way to stop myself from being consumed by my own storm. Everything was neat and orderly before her.

This whole time while my mind is out of control, I'm running with so much focus it's as if that chatter and panic isn't even happening. I finally reach her at the opening of a wooded area, and I tackle her to the ground. I wonder if she would have hid from me if she'd made it into the woods or if she would have kept running to the club.

I flip her over onto her back and straddle her. I'm destroying the lingerie I gave her. The silk is streaked with dirt. I destroy everything I touch.

*This is why we can't have nice things*, my mind taunts. And Macy is such a nice thing—far nicer than I could ever deserve.

"I'll scream. They'll hear me," she pants, her terrified gaze holding mine.

Another roll of thunder. Closer. It's closer. It's coming for me. It's coming to consume us. Maybe I won't have to do anything at all. Maybe the storm will just take us both.

"At a BDSM club? Do you think they'll come rescue you? Do you think they'll even register a scream as actual duress?"

I can see the lights from the main resort. In between the distant rumbles I almost think I hear laughter carrying on the wind. I don't know if I'm finally going completely mad —if the laughter is my own inner demons—or if we're closer to the main club than I thought. *Could* she scream? Would they hear her? Would they recognize it as true duress and not a power game some couple is playing on the grounds?

But I just glare down at her, willing her to buy into the confidence I don't feel right now. She wilts under me, and something inside me cracks open. I don't want things to be this way with her. I don't want her afraid of me. I like Weird Facts Macy, the girl who tells me the difference in fine and bone china. The one who knows arcane trivia about crown molding, which I'm sure she does.

I want her sharp mind and determination mixed with her sweetness. I want her to give herself to me, to surrender like she did earlier in the night. But that moment feels so far away from this one and impossible to reclaim now.

My gaze drifts down her body, and I notice her hand covering her belly as though she's protecting something. It's a fragile place on the body, but my attention up until now has been on her face. My eyes go to hers and back to where her hand shields her stomach.

Her eyes widen and I'm sure mine comically mirror hers. Her face is so expressive. I can read her like one of the books in her library. The words flit across her face as I look at her. Could she already be carrying my child?

How would she know this soon? But wouldn't it be a natural thing to fear? I took her virginity tonight in the most dramatic way with no protection and no birth control. Of course she'd fear she might be pregnant.

*Don't read too much into it.* I can't allow myself to be clouded by this possibility, I already feel too out of control. There are already too many variables and too many things broken beyond repair.

"Please," she whispers, tears streak down her face as lightning lights up the sky. I can see now that I've gotten Jack's blood all over her, all over that perfect pure white gown. I taint everything I touch. I destroy everything I touch.

Is she afraid I'll kill her? The woman who might be carrying my child? Isn't she right to fear that when even I don't know for sure?

Is she afraid I'll rape her? After killing Jack for the same crime? I don't want to ask these questions. I can't stand to hear her say just how big of a monster she thinks I am.

I'm breathing hard as I stare down at her, trying to find the words to erase all of this. I know I don't deserve her. I could never deserve her. She'll never look at me with anything but fear.

A dark thing inside me whispers to kill her. It's too late for us. She will always look at me with fear and revulsion. She will always try to get away from me. We can never be normal. She can't be the Mrs. Black I need to show the world, the image I want them to see. This was a stupid way to do this. I could just hire a woman to be Mrs. Black. I could find a gold digger and give her what she wants.

What's one more lie? But I wanted Macy. I wanted her. I let myself believe that we shared some desire together and that we could be somehow on the same team. Why did I let myself believe something so fucking stupid? It would be mercy to kill her now, to spare her the constant terror of my presence.

But what if she is carrying my child? She can't know this soon. That's impossible. She doesn't know. She's not pregnant. It takes more than a few hours. Even if she would become pregnant from tonight if left to nature, she's not pregnant now, in this exact moment. It's only potential. It's not real yet. It can still be undone. She can be undone. We can be undone.

I look down at her as time freezes between us, and I feel how cool it is for the first time as the winds pick up and the storm relentlessly rolls in. The thunder and lightning are coming closer together like something about to be born, and I feel the energy crackle the air. Goosebumps pop out over Macy's arms and I both want to kill her and protect her in this moment. I want to wrap her in a blanket to keep her warm. And then I want to kill her again because it feels too unsafe to feel anything so soft or kind.

A sharp, ragged breath leaves me as I say the only words that come to me. They are desperate, urgent words. They come out harsh and crazed, but I say them as our gazes lock.

"Tell me you see me. Tell me you're *with* me."

I don't know where that came from. Of all the things to say. No "let me explain", which might have sounded reasonable. No threats, which would be normal for me. *Tell me you see me. Tell me you're with me.*

What the fuck? These are impossible things to ask for, like asking Santa for world peace.

Something in her expression changes. And then a miracle happens. Somehow those stupid words have shifted things. She doesn't struggle. She doesn't scream. She doesn't pull away. She raises up with the small range of motion I've allowed her, and then her mouth is on mine.

It's not some *appease your captor* kiss. It's not a kiss of seduction. It's raw and electric. I respond to her, my hands taking her face into mine, my fingers moving through her hair as I deepen the kiss.

I shove the silk up her thigh, stroking her skin until her legs fall open for me, and a small shuddering moan escapes her. "Please," she breathes. But she's no longer begging for her life, and taking it is the farthest thing from my mind.

I struggle with my pants. This is all so fucking wrong. I'm covered in Jack's blood. She's covered in Jack's blood. There are streaks of dirt all over her, all over me, and we're about to what? Rut like a couple of animals outside?

The rain starts to fall on us as I slide inside her. "Macy," I say the word like a prayer. I don't know what just happened between us, but something has changed. And I have no idea how or why. What could have been so special about those words? They were only words. And I just killed a man. Something I remind her of with the blood we both now wear.

If she gets pregnant tonight, will it be from the big public display earlier, or this private moment between us? I drive into her wildly, like something possessed. I'm completely out of control in this moment, but she's with me. She's *with* me.

What does this mean? What do I want it to mean? I can't think. All I can do is feel her velvet softness, the sweet wetness that tells me she is absolutely with me in this moment. The whimpers and murmurs, the way she clutches at my shirt, as though just trying to hold on for the ride.

The storm swirls in full force around us. The harder I fuck her, the harder the rain comes down, the louder the thunder, the closer the lightning. It doesn't escape me that this storm could actually kill us because we're too stupid to move this indoors. But it's too late. Both of us are too close.

We're too on the edge of an ending and a beginning, a death
and a birth, and the hope that there's something happening
now that will change everything for the better.

She shrieks into the night, but it's not for help. And even
if it were, everyone has gone inside to escape the raging
storm. I follow quickly behind her, letting out a long shuddering breath as I cover my body with hers, trying to protect
her from the elements.

She continues to grip me as our breathing returns to
normal. I pull her destroyed gown back down over her, my
hand shaking. It clings to her in the rain. I zip up and then I
rise and pick her up and carry her back to the house. I know
she doesn't have the energy right now to run. I don't have the
energy to run with her in my arms.

A lightning bolt comes down and strikes a tree not thirty
feet from where we are. I hurry to get us to the safety of shelter. The odds lightning will strike again so nearby are slim,
but I feel the adrenaline buzzing through me from the close
call. Macy doesn't know just how close. Her head is
burrowed against my neck to escape the unrelenting rain.

I'm breathing hard when I get us both inside. I strip the
wet gown off her and start a fire in the fireplace. I've never
been more grateful for a quick start log already in the grate.
It's one that actually does quick start. A single match has the
fire roaring to life. I leave her sitting in front of it, wet and
shivering, trying to get warm and go get her a towel from the
nearest bathroom.

I'm sure I'm cold, too, but I don't feel it. "Are you going to
run from me again?"

She looks up. "N-no, Master." I think the stutter is more
from cold than fear. At least that's what I tell myself.

I get down next to her, so that we're eye level. "Colin. I'm
Colin to you."

We've shared an intimacy deeper than sex tonight. She's

on my team now. No one has ever really been on my team before. I have staff. I have people who fear me, people who obey me, but I don't have anyone who is truly *with* me.

Only now, maybe I do. I don't understand what changed out there, and maybe I don't need to.

I can no longer see her as some piece of property. As appealing as the idea of owning Macy was, the idea of having her as a true partner, someone who has seen my worst and chooses me anyway, that's far greater. To have a confidante.

Macy's face falls a little. What the...? Does she want...? But then I understand. She thinks I'm going to become some romance hero on her. That we'll have sweet tender sex with candlelight and rose petals. That those darker fantasies she harbors and can't show anyone but me will go back to being unexpressed fantasies.

This woman. I feel the smirk edge up. "The rain didn't wash the kink off me.

But when we aren't playing, I'm Colin."

She nods. I wish I knew what she was thinking.

I turn to go to the dungeon so I can deal with Jack's body. I had a plan, and my mind goes back to the plan... leaving him in the middle of the rainforest, to be discovered or not discovered after the animals have gotten to him.

Macy's voice stops me. "So... I'm not a sacrifice anymore?"

I turn back to her. "You're just... mine." If she thinks I'm going to let her go... I'm not that man, but I don't want her to be my prisoner. "Traditionally a sacrifice dies, and you're still here."

I don't know why I felt the need to add those words at the end. If anyone is a sacrifice tonight, it's Jack. But he's a sacrifice, not to some god, but to my own fury which has been only moderately appeased. I wish I'd had more time with him. But I couldn't do all the things I wanted to do with Macy there. Jack got mercy, and it pisses me off that the piece of shit who touched my sister, who hurt her, would get such an easy death in the end.

Macy watches me, and I can practically read her thoughts again. We both know she almost died tonight. I was so close to convincing myself it would be good for her to die, a kindness somehow. But then she saw me.

I look away. What is this awful feeling eating away at my gut? Is that guilt? Fucking guilt? I didn't know I could feel guilt for anything. Is it shame? Again, not something I thought I could feel.

"I'm going to take care of the body. Once you get warmed up you should take a hot shower and go to bed. Leave the gown. I'll get rid of it. It's evidence."

She nods. "Colin? I wanted someone to see me, too."

"I do see you, Macy." It's the only thing that saved her life tonight. And then I leave her because I can't spend another minute in this uncomfortable moment with all these feelings I don't know how to feel.

# 28

## MACY

I watch him go down the stairs and I sit staring at the fire trying to process everything that's happened since I woke. I find I can't sit still. I can't stand to just sit here while he... what? Chops up a body? And with what? IS he going to chop it up?

I hear a lot of sounds I can't fully decipher coming up from the dungeon. He left the door open. I keep waiting to hear a chainsaw, but I don't. Instead I hear a strange sliding sound. It sounds heavy. When I see him again, he's pulled Jack's plastic-wrapped body on some sort of wheeled thing, like a gurney but lower to the ground. The body is strapped on and the wheels can be folded in, which I imagine they were as he dragged him up the stairs. Now that he's on a level flat plane, the wheels are out, making it easy to move the body.

"W-what if you get caught?" This feels like such a stupid thing to say. How many people has he killed? This certainly looks like he knows what he's doing.

"I won't," Colin says, sounding far more confident than I feel about this.

"Colin...?"

He looks up. "Yeah?"

"When will you be back?" The storm has settled down to just heavy rain, but I'm still worried.

"By sunrise. Get cleaned up and go back to sleep."

We both know I could escape while he's gone. He could choose to chain me up in the dungeon to prevent that, but he doesn't. He either doesn't care or is absolutely confident that what happened outside earlier changes everything somehow.

And doesn't it?

I just nod, and he leaves. I can't help going back downstairs. He's already done a lot of the cleanup. All the plastic wrap is gone, rolled up neatly and duct taped closed. Where is he disposing that? How is he disposing it? I close my eyes and take a deep breath. He's not going to share this kind of information with me. I know he knows what he's doing and deep down I know Jack isn't the first. And I know they weren't all men who did things as bad as what I think Jack may have done to his sister. Can I really be the woman who looks the other way while her husband does these terrible things?

It didn't escape me that Jack thought he was being killed for a business betrayal and not something far more personal. I go upstairs and carefully pick up the silk robe and take it to the second floor with me. I don't even look at the gown. I know it's ruined beyond repair, but the robe at least, is still perfect.

The robe still feels like "Before Macy". It's me before what happened outside. Before everything changed completely and forever. It's telling that I feel like there was still a "Before Macy" when I watched him kill Jack and ran up the stairs, and the thing that splits time for me is what happened outside. I go upstairs and lay the robe on the bed and go into the bathroom.

I stare at my reflection for a long time. I look wild. Jack's blood was all over the gown, so I know it was on me, too. But the rain washed all of that clean. And any mud that might have been on me, Colin dried off with the towel. I look and feel too clean for everything that's happened tonight.

Am I being stupid for not running? I'm no longer wearing the tracking bracelet, and Colin's distracted covering up a crime. I make excuses for myself like where would I go? Where is my passport? I have no money to travel by myself. I can't just hide out in Costa Rica, I have to go home. Is Colin not concerned I'll run? Or did he just forget he removed the bracelet?

I could turn him in and get a free trip home. I could run to the main resort, tell the truth about everything, and get to some imagined safety. But it feels like too deep a betrayal, not only of him, but of myself.

I'm not sure if I love Colin or if I can love him. It's too soon to know something like that. I'm not sure if he can love me, but I can't deny whatever thing flowed between us outside in the rain.

*Tell me you see me. Tell me you're with me.*

When he echoed my own thoughts of less than an hour before right back at me, I could no longer deny what I felt. It doesn't matter if it's right or wrong. He's the only man who can ever truly get me. I feel like the only woman who could ever truly get him. And so that's the way it is.

For better or worse.

~

I HOPE you enjoyed THE SACRIFICE. If you're new to my work, please consider joining my newsletter. In exchange you'll get a free story available exclusively to subscribers: https://kittythomas.com/free-book/

IF YOU'RE new to this world and haven't had a chance to read The Proposal yet (Livia's book), be sure to check that one out! You can read the first chapter free at my website: https://kittythomas.com/book/the-proposal/

THE PROPOSAL IS ALSO available in audiobook, narrated by Meg Sylvan and Sebastian York.

THE PROPOSAL:

I GOT in over my head.

I bit off more than I could chew.

And now my fate is sealed to the most ruthless man I know.

Two hundred and fifty guests. They think they know what's happening today. But they don't have a clue.

My wedding day. But it's so much more than that.

FOR A LIST of all my titles, please go here: https://kittythomas.com/reading-order-for-new-readers/

TO HEAR BEHIND-THE-SCENES information from The Sacrifice and what's coming next, turn the page...

. . .

THANK you for reading and supporting my work!

Kitty ^.^

# BEHIND THE SCENES WITH KITTY

Hello my little Godiva chocolates with white chocolate drizzle,

If you're new to me, that might be a bit much for a reader endearment, but it is what it is. Before I get into this author's note, I do want to reassure you that there is more Macy and Colin coming, and I'll get more into that a little further into the note.

I didn't know when I started writing The Proposal that I was writing a duet. It wasn't until I got to the end, the scene at the kink club where Colin and Soren are speaking and Soren offers him something innocent that he can keep forever with conditions that I realize Macy is going to get all her dark twisted fantasies fulfilled after all.

I love the idea of Colin and Macy because they are both the exact same amount of wrong. Colin may come from the darker side of the spectrum and Macy may come from the lighter side, but they meet in the middle.

I'm also not inordinately into "virgin stories". That's not

necessarily my kink... the innocent virginal lamb meets the big bad wolf. It's just how it happened. With The Proposal, Livia isn't actually a literal virgin, but because of the set-up of the book, it ends up having that same sort of energy. And in many ways she is a virgin because she certainly has never been with three men at once. And waiting for the wedding night to consummate continues the theme and keeps the tension high.

The whole idea of virginity, while it comes with it's own issues, at its root, it's really about being initiated into a new experience either as the initiate or as the initiator. It's about a rite of passage with a defining act that moves you from one state of being into another. And I think this is why when we have two virgins getting together it doesn't have the same energy as someone experienced and a virgin because with two virgins, no one is the initiator, and we don't get that polarity. It's just two nervous people awkwardly fumbling.

Even though Livia wasn't a virgin in The Proposal, all the men being in on the situation and all of them having a lot of experience and planning to consummate with her all at once on the wedding night, sets up this initator/initated dynamic.

So since we sort of got on the virgin kick with The Proposal, the energy if not the literal thing itself, I decided to continue that pattern into The Sacrifice with Macy. I loved the idea of Macy as this woman who has such a filthy mind but just hasn't had the opportunity to test it out yet.

We've all had a point in our lives where someone who supposedly was older or wiser than us or more experienced thought they knew us better than we did or thought we didn't know what we wanted or what we liked because how can you know if you haven't done it? Sometimes we do know.

This comes up a lot with whether or not women want

children as well as our sexual likes and dislikes, as though we're complete blank slates and have to try absolutely everything out first to know whether we'd be into it or not. I like that Macy is into it before she's even tried it and that Colin finds the person who isn't pretending.

All these other women he's been with are so experienced. But they aren't into it. By contrast, she's so inexperienced, but she is.

The story started to build around The Sacrifice as a metaphor, and then into an actual ritual event that ended up in many ways mirroring the opening scene where she's fantasizing.

I love the way the book opens because if you've read me, it's not hard for you to imagine that yep, this is actually what's somehow happening right now. If you'd read The Proposal first you might have tiny little twinges that something is off or doesn't logistically add up in that scene from what you already know. But for the most part you're buying it.

And then the phone rings.

I hate the "it was all a dream" plot device, but I think you'll forgive me if it's the opening scene. It's a small surprise that doesn't feel like a betrayal because we're just getting started... especially as we build toward creating a version of this very scene for the end of the book. Because if you've read me much you know I love the story mirror.

I got really blocked on this book for a long time. It took me over a year to write it, during which time I took a break to write Berserker because I was so stalled out. And part of the issue was that I realized this is two books, not one. I was so married (no pun intended, ok maybe a little bit) to the idea that this was a duet, that I didn't realize that Colin and Macy require more than one book.

This book is literally "The Sacrifice". That's what it is. It's how Macy came to be with Colin. It's their origin story. But there's more. I could have put it all in one book but it would have been an unnaturally long book with weird pacing issues.

I could have tried to cram 60,000 more words worth of fiction into 10,000 and rushed the ending. But I decided instead to just finish the duet and then write another book or novella that isn't exactly part of the duet, but continues Macy and Colin's story. I will likely link all three together. Or, I may put it into a new series revolving around The Silver Circle.

For this reason I wasn't able to have the "Livia finds out about things" scene because that's part of a much larger plot and story. I hate cliffhangers, and I don't feel I've written one. Yes there's more story and there's a subplot I didn't wrap up because I can't in this book. You'll understand when we get there.

I'm not sure when this next book is coming out, but I try to write all my books as stand alones even when part of a larger world so you aren't "tied to" a long series or a big book commitment and having to remember everything or being frustrated by cliffhangers. Did I mention I hate cliffhangers? That was one reason I was blocked so long because I hated the idea that I'd have to do another book to do this right and how do I do that without making readers feel they've been set up with a cliffhanger? The solution to me was to focus on wrapping up the main point of the book, indicated by the title, then start fresh into a new story with them.

Anyway I think that's about all the rambling I can do about this one.

Thank you so much for reading/listening to and supporting my work! Be sure to subscribe to my newsletter at Kittythomas.com to know about all the things and for a free book.

Kitty out.

# ACKNOWLEDGMENTS

Thank you to the following people for their help with The Sacrifice:

Robin Ludwig Design Inc. Cover design. Beautiful cover as always!

Lori Jackson for her amazing teaser graphics.